PRAISE FOR
"BOSTON, MY BLISSFUL WINTER"

The keen eye and pen of French author Alain Briottet deftly sketches the luminous beauty of Boston's soul in winter. I became viscerally engaged and surprised by his character's discovery of the cityscape, its neighborhoods and the interior spaces where Bostonians retreat from the cold, seeking companionship and shelter. This book marvelously reveals the elusive and timeless qualities of our town that led me to seek out the unexpected during all its seasons.

Bárbara de Bragança
Former President of the Alliance Française de Boston-Cambridge
Trustee of the French Cultural Center, Boston, Massachusetts

The keen observer in *Boston, My Blissful Winter* introduces us not only to specific Boston locations and neighborhoods but also to a variety of denizens, iconic individuals, young and elderly, ranging from Brahmins to French Canadians. Challenging weather and musical motifs enhance the unforgettable portraits, creating an atmosphere at once nostalgic and palpable. The prose reads like poetry, and the vivid descriptions remain as relevant today as when they were written.

Lia Poorvu
Retired Lecturer, Tufts University
Officier des Palmes Académiques

A perfect jewel box of short stories. Alain Briottet created his characters with the eye of a portrait painter. His stories unfold like short films expressing a humanity and universality that will appeal to all those who cherish memories of a city they love.

Betsey Buddy
Retired French teacher, Greenwich, Connecticut

The charming recollections of a Frenchman's first encounters with Boston society. The young banking intern recounts his impressions of familiar places, from the Ritz to the Blue Diner, with original perceptions and affectionate humor. Deftly rendered into English from the original French, this is a book to savor and return to again and again to revisit a favorite story.

Mary Louise Burke
President, Boston/Strasbourg Sister City Association

During his posting to the French Consulate in Boston, Ambassador Alain Briottet came to observe and befriend neighbors of Beacon Hill with whom he came to feel a common bond. Now, in twelve luminous stories, he shares observations and insights of encounters, that are often brief, and that may mark you permanently. Briottet's compassion and gift for rich friendships provide moving portrayals that belie the stereotype of frigid, puritanical Brahmins. Paulette Boudrot's admirable translation of his lyrical prose reveals that though winter in Boston may be cold, the lives of the inhabitants are decidedly not.

Margaret Collins Weitz
Author, Sisters in the Resistance:
How Women Fought to Free France 1940–1945

The magic of a winter in Boston is here, revealed in its many hues. Each story presents a different situation affording the chance to experience the tiniest wonder—changes in the atmosphere, footsteps in the snow, the slant of a winter sun—all captured in the author's crystal-clear, thoughtful, and detailed writing. He makes us see and feel what he has seen and felt, offering us the fabric of a life that we discover to be our own.

Alain Malraux
Playwright, Paris

In sensitive, lyrical prose, these short stories highlight the ephemeral nature of time, as experienced by a young intern who spends a winter working at a large bank in Boston. The parallels between his experience and that of the author, a career diplomat stationed in Boston during the 1980s, are unmistakable. It is the contrast between the harmony of nature and the disruption of the real world that is the strength of this collection; these stories make you think about life.

Phillipe Martial
Honorary Director, Library & Archives, French Senate, Paris

While reading *Boston, un hiver si court*, I hear a resuscitated Talleyrand telling me that "Those who did not live before September 11 don't know the sweetness of living." My dear Boston in the eighties is masterfully summoned by Alain Briottet, not so much through an evocation of sweetness than by the melancholy and understated sharpness of its vignettes, which create a stirring poetry.

André Citroën
International Financial Consultant, Paris

ALSO BY ALAIN BRIOTTET

Sine Die, Gross-Born en Poméranie, Editions Illador, Versailles (2016)

Boston, un hiver si court, Editions du Rocher, Paris (2007)

L'esprit des lois et la constitution américaine, Lecture at the Boston Public Library, Editions Bilingue, Société Historique Franco-Américaine (1988)

To Denise
Joyeux Anniversaire
de mariage
Signy !! Paulette

BOSTON
My Blissful Winter

Memories of the 1980s

ALAIN BRIOTTET

Translated from French by Paulette Boudrot

Edited by Ellen Albanese

Paulette Boudrot

ISBN: 978-1-941416-21-1 (paperback)

ISBN: 978-1-941416-22-8 (electronic book)

Library of Congress Catalog Number: 2019941455

P.R.A. Publishing

P.O. Box 211701

Martinez, GA 30917

www.prapublishing.com

Cover design by Michelle Williams.

Interior design by Medlar Publishing Solutions Pvt Ltd., India.

Printed in the United States of America

This is a work of fiction, except for references to historical figures and landmarks.

For my Boston friends

EPIGRAPH

Twelve below zero this morning. The pipes in the kitchen and the guest bathroom are frozen. The arctic sea smoke was thick and steaming over the ocean after the sun rose. I sat down and wrote a poem very fast … this is what has not happened until today and always seems like a "possession." I have a little joke which is that only the rich can afford to stay in New England in winter … the poor go to Florida. My heat bill was $250 for December. I just paid the plumber $69 for fixing the hot water heater, and now, of course, there'll be more to pay for unfreezing the pipes.

May Sarton
The House by the Sea: A Journal
W.W. Norton and Company, New York/London

TABLE OF CONTENTS

1

LATE ONE SUNDAY
AFTERNOON IN WINTER

It was snowing lightly when I left the home of my friends the Wicks. Small swirls of snowflakes were fluttering down on West Cedar Street. The sky over Beacon Hill, reflecting the barely hidden sun, was turning pink. The air was mild, and the falling snowflakes invited me to join in their dance. There was something peaceful, carefree, and leisurely about this late winter afternoon. I didn't want the day to end.

I decided to walk to Commonwealth Avenue, where I lived. I turned onto Pinckney Street and started down Beacon Hill, not knowing yet if I would turn left to browse along Charles Street, or if I would take the long way toward the banks of the frozen Charles River by turning right. Lots of people were ambling along Charles Street. Joggers were weaving around pedestrians, sometimes darting between the cars crawling along the street covered with a thick carpet of snow. Some strollers would stop in front of the store windows decorated for Christmas, or in front of the pine trees bundled together on the sidewalk. They were from Maine and were being sold at a discount.

By the time I reached Charles Street, I had decided that it was too late to go all the way to the river and take a detour by the Esplanade Hatch Shell. Instead I walked along Charles Street and stopped for a while at the Dolce Momento Café. I went there almost every Sunday for lunch and to read the newspapers. Today, the Wicks' invitation had changed my schedule, but I still wanted to end my afternoon at the café.

The Dolce Momento reminded me of a large European-style café. It's located at the bottom of Beacon Hill at the intersection of Charles and Chestnut Streets. I like the ambience there. The atmosphere is similar to being in a lively classroom created by the many students who stopped by. Some came to study, others came to chat, but they all came to eat soup served with bread and butter and to enjoy a real meal for only a few dollars.

Because I prefer to look out the window, I usually sat on the banquette along the far wall perpendicular to the street. This corner seemed to be reserved for those who came to read the newspapers left there by the café's owners. Several copies of the *Boston Globe's* thick Sunday edition, and the *Boston Herald* were left abandoned on the tables. Once in a while you could find sections of the *New York Times* left behind by a forgetful customer. The conversations and the laughter didn't bother those reading the newspapers; they just ignored it. The longer they stayed, the more their concentration increased, reading their newspapers while distractedly eating soup that had become cold, and then they would carelessly push the wrinkled pages aside. I found this American habit distasteful, and promised myself that I would behave differently. I would carefully unfold and refold the newspapers, and I would replace the pages in their proper order following the page numbers. Unlike the focused readers who spent a long time with their newspapers, I only scanned them, generally only reading the headlines. I was more interested in the Sunday supplements of the *Boston Globe* and the *New York Times*, if I could find them.

I liked the literary and travel sections. And I always read the weather forecast for the coming week. Like most Bostonians, I shared the obsession of always wanting to know what the meteorologist would predict for the morning. While still in bed, I would dial the weather bureau's telephone number, 936-1234, to listen to the forecast for that day. Also, from my office window, I often glanced at the giant barometer on top of the Old Hancock Tower. It operates like a traffic light. A blue light means a sunny day and a clear sky; a glowing red light means rain or snow; and when the light starts flashing, it means changing weather, *"flashing blue, flashing red!"* The Old Hancock Tower's flashing lights determined my schedule, my free time, and perhaps even my life. What pleased me most at the Dolce Momento was to be able to look out at the street from my seat at the end of the banquette facing Charles Street. Unfortunately, that place was sometimes already occupied by serious newspaper readers. I liked to look at all the people passing by and, on some Sundays, recognized some I had already met since arriving in Boston, or some I had simply passed in the street. Many were from Beacon Hill, but not all were Brahmins.

It was easy for me to spot the people from Beacon Hill because they had certain mannerisms: they always walked at a certain pace and dressed in a certain manner. They lived in the neighborhood, and the streets were familiar to them; strolling would mean they were not from Beacon Hill. I had already noticed that they dressed in full, long coats, very rarely in parkas or windbreakers, and they wore a variety of headgear, from balaclavas to flat caps for men, from wool hats pulled down over their ears to felt hats for women. Some of them carried huge umbrellas, moving slowly and cautiously, careful to avoid the cracks on the cobblestone sidewalks. These were usually the ones dressed as if they were going to a fancy reception. And black seemed *de rigeur* as a color of choice for any type of fashion accessory. In spite of the uneven pavement and the cracked sidewalks, no one seemed bothered by the snow. In fact, it seemed to stimulate them; they appeared attracted by it as accomplices to its games and greedy for its pleasures.

I could guess by their pace and by their attire whether they were going toward the Public Garden, eager to traipse on the pristine snow where scampering squirrels had left enigmatic arabesque designs, or whether, after crossing the Public Garden through a shortcut by the mounted George Washington statue, they were headed to Boylston or Newbury Streets, toward the big hotels for afternoon tea or dinner.

Once, a slightly older couple, dressed as if they were going to a reception, attracted my attention. They were standing at the crosswalk of Charles and Chestnut Streets, probably waiting for a taxi. He was rather tall, holding an enormous bright blue golf umbrella over their heads. He was wearing a large brimmed hat, and the scarf knotted under the collar of his raincoat gave his silhouette an air of eccentric elegance. She held onto his arm and seemed very petite standing next to him. She was wearing a long hooded black cape that didn't even protect her face.

Then I realized it was the Alberts, Mildred and James. I had met them at a reception given to launch a new financial product. The director at the Bank of Boston had invited the bank's foreign personnel to introduce them to their important customers. I was the only French employee at the time. Shortly afterward, I was invited to their home. They lived in a small house on Acorn Street in the heart of Beacon Hill. The Alberts were a part of Boston society, and many Brahmins had crowded into their small parlor that evening. Mildred had spent her career in fashion and had become one of the city's prominent personalities. That night, I met Mrs. Caron Lebrun, one of Boston's best chroniclers, who subsequently became a friend. Caron told me all about Mildred. It was a wonderful story. Mildred would never have been admitted to the Beacon Hill society: she didn't have the correct ethnic background; her appearance wasn't appropriate; she hadn't attended the best schools, and she hadn't married well. However, the Brahmins had accepted her, and treated her with respect. Better yet, as she became a dignified and serene older woman, she gained their affection and they admired her. They organized a gala dinner at the Ritz to celebrate her 80th birthday, which is the ultimate sign of esteem and respect. That night, all of Boston's exclusive society was in the grand ballroom. The Brahmins wanted to show their gratitude to this woman who had helped make their city famous; they had adopted her and made her part of their circle.

When I looked at Mildred from the Dolce Momento, her petite silhouette enveloped in her long black cape, her face radiating in the reflected blue light of the umbrella, I sensed how happy she was at her husband's side. I thought to myself that she certainly was distinguished and graceful. I recalled her smile, the soft intonation of her voice that had preserved something timid and juvenile from her youth, her simple mannerisms when she greeted me at her home, her unaffected gestures. All these traits could only charm the Bostonians. But I wondered if this was enough to conquer them and really become part of their in-group?

Certainly something more was needed: a perfected skill, an imposing demeanor, a success beyond our imagination. She needed something more to help them forget her birth in a Russian Jewish family before 1917, to forget her modest beginnings at the Massachusetts General Hospital, where she helped those with a broken leg or fractured foot to walk again. They needed to forget she had no degrees, a marriage that brought her neither fortune nor influential relationships, a physical attractiveness without beauty.

Only the qualities that professional etiquette instructors require could explain the stature she attained in the city's society. Bostonians are too objective to be taken in by sentimental infatuation.

Her career and success began when one of her physical therapy patients at Massachusetts General Hospital asked her very seriously, "Instead of working on physical therapy, why don't you teach my daughter to walk properly? She will be turning 18 years old soon and will be presented to Boston society." Mildred seized the opportunity immediately, collected some money, rented space for a workshop, and formed "The Modern Academy." There she gave lessons in poise and manners to young girls from elite Boston families who were making their debut into society. This "Modern Academy" became "The Art Model Agency," with fashion houses in Boston and New York competing for her models. Her classes encompassed sewing, modeling, poise, and fashion. It was a success from the very beginning. It was Mildred Albert herself, in her direct and precise manner, who organized all the fashion shows.

5

By the time she was 30, she was managing her own business. According to Caron Lebrun, more than 20,000 young women from Boston had taken her classes.

At the height of her career, in spite of the many offers and invitations she received, Mildred decided to stay in Boston, unlike many others who measured their success by establishing themselves in New York.

When she decided to close the agency, she sold her school, but continued to work by writing fashion articles for newspapers, and appearing on television. In addition, she began inviting her acquaintances from Boston's society, who had entertained her over the years, to her small coachman's house on Acorn Street. The Brahmins came to bear witness to her strong will, her tenacity, her work ethic, her perfectionism: all the virtues they hold in esteem. To the Brahmins, Mildred Albert had become one of them.

Emerging from my reverie, I noticed the Alberts were no longer there. They must have taken a taxi. Although both were advanced in years, it did not prevent them from accepting invitations to receptions and dinners. Their need to socialize seemed to increase as their remaining years decreased. Going out was like delaying that final encounter, which they did not consider very dignified.

Jeremy Widman was going by the café window now. I met him last Thanksgiving at the home of mutual friends, a married couple who were professors like Jeremy. Before teaching at MIT, Jeremy was an economics professor at Harvard for several years. He had invited me to his home for a drink.

Jeremy walked at a rapid pace, looking straight ahead. He was bareheaded, dressed in blue jeans, and wore a leather aviator jacket with the fur collar turned up against his neck.

He rented a two-bedroom apartment in one of those buildings at the bottom of Beacon Hill called "the flats" that were built at the beginning of the twentieth century. The rents there were lower than at the top of the hill, but the condominiums on the top floors had a magnificent view. Jeremy Widman's apartment, located on Brimmer Street, was one of those.

His windows faced the park, and you could see the white sails of the boats from the sailing club scattered along the Charles River next to the Long-fellow Bridge. Beyond that was a view of the Massachusetts Institute of Technology (MIT) domes.

Brimmer Street is on the border of The Hill, and although technically he lived on The Hill, he had been on the Harvard faculty, and he had all the appropriate qualifications, Jeremy Widman seemed to live on the fringe of Beacon Hill society.

Was it because he too, like Mildred, was of Jewish ancestry? Was it because he wasn't wealthy, even though he was well paid by MIT and sup-plemented his income by writing political articles for economic reviews and publications? Was it because he wasn't married and was always seen alone? The truth is that Jeremy Widman was not part of Beacon Hill soci-ety simply because he did not want to be part of it. The people of The Hill ignored him, and no longer invited him. He had decided to live there because he liked the neighborhood, the tranquility, the security of a res-idential community, the proximity to downtown Boston and its major streets: Boylston, Columbus, and Tremont. When walking home from Cambridge after teaching, his pace was usually slower, as if he were admir-ing the shining hill and its brick houses reflected in the setting sun, as if Boston's red bricks were on fire.

Jeremy Widman felt at home on Beacon Hill. He felt protected from others and from himself, free in the middle of his puritanical and intolerant neighbors. He lived alone in his overly furnished apartment and didn't want to be separated from the many items he had inherited from his parents. He said he would sell them when he retired. That wouldn't be soon because he had just turned forty and looked ten years younger.

Not very tall, he stayed thin, was well proportioned, and walked with a bouncy gait. He had a full face and exuded good health. When compli-mented on his physical condition, he would say that he ate little and walked a lot. I thought to myself that Jeremy must also go to the gym and exercise to maintain his athletic, muscular figure. But he never mentioned these intensive and regular workouts. In fact, it seemed to me that he didn't want others to know about them.

I discovered his secret totally by accident. As I was going to a dinner, invited by some friends who lived locally, I found myself face to face with Jeremy Widman. He had a gym bag in his hand and was in front of an athletic club on Columbus Avenue. The workout rooms in the basement can be seen through the windows facing the street. They're part of the same building that has a bar and a restaurant on the first floor and a performance hall in the back. Judging from the young people going in, it seemed that the club was used mostly by yuppies from Bay Village and the South End.

"I see you like to walk," I said to him.

"One of Boston's charms is that you can walk a lot. It's easy to walk and even run. That's why I don't have a car. And it helps me to relax, loosen up, and stretch my legs after my classes."

"But I would imagine MIT has magnificent sports facilities."

"Yes, but coming all the way here gives me more exercise. And I like the change of scenery and neighborhoods every once in a while."

As Jeremy was going toward the club entrance, he pointed to a small sign stuck to the window, and laughingly said, "It's also more entertaining!"

On the small sign, above a picture of Marilyn Monroe by Andy Warhol, was written "Tonight, Jimmy James, in person."

Jeremy Widman stepped through the door, happy to find his weights, his barbells, the trapeze and ropes, the stationary skiing and climbing machines. He disappeared into his club as into a labyrinth of lust.

I felt like staying a little longer at Dolce Momento. I felt good there, sheltered in the warmth, an observation post during a lull in the storm. I had been there for two hours now and it was almost evening. I had done a lot of daydreaming and little reading. In fact, I didn't want to leave until I saw a certain pedestrian who passed by every Sunday at around five o'clock. Seeing her meant that I should go home too, but of course, her appearance meant something else. I waited for her as if I had a date, my heart anxious and nervous.

My gaze wandered toward the street, from the Commons to the Public Garden, to Beacon Street. In the falling darkness, I was searching among the fewer pedestrians for this person who, at the stroke of five, would become my imaginary date.

My heart was pounding. She was arriving.

One couldn't tell that this old woman had something that set her apart from the other pedestrians. She came toward Charles Street, having finished her walk in the Public Garden, and now she was going home. She was dressed in black, and her long cloth coat (it couldn't have been fur) hung to her feet. She wore boots from another era, and her hat was made of two different styles: a black wool hood that covered half her face to protect her from the wind, and a large felt brim, also black. She wore a long white silk scarf in a bizarre fashion, as a stole around her neck and shoulders. Her whole getup, her slow and majestic pace, the smallest details of her appearance captivated my attention. But she seemed indifferent to what was going on around her; she seemed completely absorbed in her thoughts.

I had met her once before at Marika's, an antiques dealer on Charles Street, when she was negotiating the price of old jewelry, silver pieces, and some old paintings. Overhearing her conversation with the dealer, I understood that she had placed something with him to be sold, and now she was eager to complete the sale because she was about to leave Boston for Maine. She told him she was going to take care of her longtime friend who was now an invalid.

Her voice was high pitched with a worldly affectation, like women born at the turn of the century. Her English was marked by a foreign accent, perhaps French. Her impatience was obvious in her voice and gestures, the way she put her gloves on with a quick and contemptuous pull. Our eyes met only briefly, but very intensely. She quickly looked away, as if to let me know I already knew enough about her. I remember especially the piercing blue of her eyes. She turned into Chestnut Street to climb the hill. I imagined that she lived in one of the houses in Louisburg Square. However, I had never seen her among any of the other residents there, not even on

Christmas night when the Brahmins took out their silver and opened their doors to their neighbors after attending the nativity service at the Church of the Advent.

Was she a boarder in a home for old people in Louisburg Square? Did she live hidden on the cold northern slope of Beacon Hill? Was she in Boston for this winter only? Or did she really live on a small island in Maine, forgotten, alone, and bitter, often looking at the fuming ocean? It was now nighttime.

Dolce Momento was empty. The waitresses were standing at the bar, taking a break before a new wave of customers arrived for dinner. Some were speaking softly among themselves; others were resting silently on their chairs, arms dangling, staring blankly into space. Outside, Charles Street was also empty and it was beginning to snow.

It was time to return to Back Bay, where I lived.

I picked up the pages of the *Boston Globe* in front of me. I concentrated on putting them together, and paid particular attention to keeping them in correct numerical order. Once this was done, I carefully folded the newspaper in two, and inserted the Sunday supplement in the middle. This Sunday was ending like all the others.

By casually perusing the newspaper, I learned that the world was in a decline, that France had not yet finished celebrating the bicentennial of 1789, that the winter would be harsh in New England, that the Commonwealth of Massachusetts was tired of its governor, and that Boston remained Boston. While folding the newspaper I felt guilty because I really hadn't read much. I should have read the news more carefully. I admitted to myself, however, that world events seemed far removed from me and not related to my life. And even if I had read more seriously, would that have changed anything for me? I had been attracted by the people who appeared in my field of vision, who make up part of my consciousness. I believed they were definitely fixed in my memory. I felt we had something in common at a moment when our lives had crossed; our souls had perhaps been opened under the shock of the unexpected meeting. Dreams had perhaps been created in our minds at that moment. Did we follow them? Did we nourish them with other dreams? Or did we stifle them under the weight of reason?

Among the unknown people I had fleetingly met, and who had suddenly become so close to me, hadn't I learned that life, this barbed-wire camp, granted me permission to exit, gave me a means to escape? Neither the old couple waiting for the taxi, nor the sporty professor from MIT, nor the lady in black from The Hill would be able to deny that life had offered them the opportunity to leave their prison, even if it were just through a Sunday afternoon in winter.

When I left Dolce Momento to go home, I didn't take the shortcut through the Public Garden. I liked going along Beacon Street better, passing in front of the Hampshire House, and going through the small spirited crowd heading toward their evening meal. People seem to eat early in Boston so they can work late into the evening. Then I turned onto Arlington Street before reaching the first numbers of Commonwealth Avenue, number 3, where I lived. After going by Harbridge House and turning onto Commonwealth Avenue I could see the Old Hancock Tower above the slanted rooftops and above the bell tower of the First Baptist Church. It was red; it meant snow. We were in store for a long night. The snow was falling heavily by the time I arrived home. It was falling on the temporary wooden steps covering the original stone staircase the owner had installed for the winter. It was falling on the two magnolia trees and the scraggly branches that framed the porch. It was falling on the neo-Gothic arches, on the silent façade, and I could see the flakes swirling, a foreboding storm in the reflection of the gas lamp lights on Commonwealth Avenue. The snowstorm would continue all night long.

Tomorrow, the city would be covered in a coat of white, resplendent in the winter sun. Tomorrow, the Old Hancock Tower would revert to the color of a bright blue sky.

Flashing blue. Flashing red. O, my dear Old Hancock Tower!

2

THE STORY OF A T-SHIRT
AND A MOTHER'S LOVE

The banks were closed on Saturday, but I had asked Liz, my secretary, to make an exception and come in to work this particular Saturday morning. I wanted her to type a short speech that I was to give at Faneuil Hall in Quincy Market at noon about an ice sculpture contest.

Because the year 1986 was the centennial celebration of the Statue of Liberty, the participants in the contest were to make ice sculptures of Frédéric Auguste Bartholdi's statue. The committee had asked the Bank of Boston, sponsors of the event, to send a representative to present the first prize. Being the only French person at the bank, it was only natural that I was chosen for this task.

I had arrived at the office early and was trying to compose my small speech, but I was having trouble finding ideas. Remembering that the Statue of Liberty was a gift from France, I wanted to focus more on this gift of friendship and its creator because I noticed that many Americans did not know or remember this aspect. I felt it necessary to emphasize the significance of the monument. Then I was stuck and couldn't get any further. I skated around the subject, always coming back to the same idea: the statue symbolizes the end of tyranny, the end of oppression, the end of servitude. This was obvious to the immigrants who had succeeded in coming to America during the last century. But what did the Statue of Liberty mean to today's generation? I kept asking the question without coming up with a good answer.

Liz had arrived by now. I heard her making noises and talking on the telephone in her office next to mine. Shortly after, still wearing her wool hat, her cheeks rosy on this icy cold February morning, she came through the door separating our two rooms. As usual, she was smiling.

"You know," I told her, "I'm very late and I haven't finished my speech. Here are the first two pages, so please start typing them now."

"I'll type what you've already written," she told me. "For the rest of it, you only need to jot down the ideas. Inspiration will come very easily after you've seen the exhibit and all the sculptures. And then, keep it simple. After all, you are only congratulating the winner."

"Yes, you're right. But there will be television cameras, and later on when I see myself stammering and stuttering, I'll regret not having been better prepared. I still have a good hour's work to do, so let me finish. I would like to be quiet now."

Liz was consistently optimistic. She said she always sought to find the good side of things, and one had to have confidence in God, who never failed to help when needed; you had to pray a lot, and only prayer would lift you up from the miseries of the world. She was convinced that daily prayer would help heal the illnesses of the body and those of the soul. As a devout member of the Christian Science Church, she never missed an opportunity to preach its doctrine.

The door between our two offices was slightly open. I glanced over and noticed little Kenneth, Liz's son, still wrapped up in his duffle coat, reluctant to enter.

Liz quickly said: "I brought Kenneth with me because I didn't have anyone to stay with him this morning, and I had promised to type your speech."

I thought I understood perfectly well the association that she made: no typed speech without Kenneth. However, I hadn't completely realized that they would accompany me to the ceremony until Liz added: "Kenneth will be very happy to see the ice sculptures. They're very famous in Boston, you know. New Englanders know how to carve ice; they've been doing it commercially for a long time. Kenneth will come with us to Faneuil Hall."

"Very well," I replied a bit nastily, "as you always bring your son everywhere you go."

I recognized immediately that this last remark was not fair on my part, and I regretted it. Even if Liz wanted to show Kenneth the ice sculptures, at least she had come to type my speech in spite of the cold and snowy Saturday morning. She was a single mother raising her small boy, so why should I blame her?

Liz became my secretary when I first arrived at the bank. She was already working there and had found this job shortly after her husband left her. That was a little more than three years ago. She made a good impression with her perfect manners, wearing a proper blouse with sleeves and a pencil skirt as advised in the current fashion magazines for "executive women." She was the daughter of a military attaché from Philadelphia, which, even in Boston, is a good reference. Her knowledge of French, which she learned as a child while her father was stationed at the American Embassy in Paris, separated her from the pack of candidates and easily earned her the position as my personal assistant.

I was pleased to have her collaboration as my secretary. I was enchanted by her enthusiasm, freshness, and the optimism she brought to everything she undertook, no doubt to better disguise her own difficulties. She continuously amused me with her spontaneous reactions, sometimes naïve in regard to people, and her critical judgments that were always inspired by Christian Science's moral teachings. I was aware that her pronouncements reflected her deep faith. As a church without clergy, Christian Scientists knew how to find propagandists like Liz who were intelligent and unremitting.

Liz and Kenneth, who had just turned five years old, lived in a small apartment on Saint Botolph Street, in a building just behind the Prudential Center. The rent was not too high, although she complained that it was equal to a good third of her salary. But she had taken this apartment for a very specific reason; from there she could be at the Christian Science Church within a few minutes.

Almost every morning she went to the lecture hall in the church to read the Bible and the writings by the church's founder, Mary Baker Eddy. On certain winter days when snowstorms forced her to take the subway, the MBTA (Massachusetts Bay Transportation Authority, or the T as it is known in Boston) and she couldn't go to church, she did her religious readings at the office. As soon as she arrived, she would read her texts, which she had glued to little blank pieces of paper and arranged in front of her like a game of cards; she read them with such a deep concentration that it astounded and exasperated me at the same time. So that she would not be disturbed, she would refuse to answer the phone and would even take the receiver off the hook, which was extremely noble on her part because she was a very curious person and loved to talk on the phone. Therefore, during those twenty minutes that Liz devoted to her spiritual exercises, my office was cut off from all contact with my superiors and with the outside world.

Although Liz read the Bible and Mary Baker Eddy every morning, she didn't read the *Christian Science Monitor* newspaper, which she rarely bought, not because she would have found it boring, but because politics didn't interest her at all. Like most people, she formed her opinions regarding events and politicians from what she saw on television and from what others told her they had seen or heard. She did make one important exception, however, and that was for Boston politicians. She was more intrigued with their personal lives than with their political views and activities, because she believed that their lives were similar to hers.

Boston politicians were like distant relatives for Liz, familiar neighbors she could meet while crossing the street, whose life experiences were similar to hers. On winter days they shoveled snow in front of their homes in

Brookline, or in Fall River, just as she did; during the summer they escaped the city's heat by going to the North Shore beaches or Cape Cod, as she did. On the 4th of July she could find them on the Hatch Shell lawn listening to popular music and watching the fireworks. And again, politicians could be standing next to her during the Columbus Day and Martin Luther King Day parades.

All year long Liz saw them, met them, and was not shy about talking to them. For example, every time she met Boston's mayor, Raymond Flynn, who often walked home as she did, she would ask him about his wife and children. Furthermore, he was a practicing Catholic, which pleased her immensely.

Even though they made up a small part of her world, Liz, with much insight, was quick to judge elected Boston officials. From the very beginning of Governor Michael Dukakis's campaign for the White House, Liz had seen the weaknesses in his candidacy. Although she considered his private life irreproachable and his frugal tendencies appealed to her, she was certain that he would not be elected. She found him to be too cold in his relationships with people and a bit too logical in his explanations. She also thought that his wife's problems could be a deterrent and would weaken his campaign. Like most Bostonians, she liked Mrs. Dukakis, whom she called "Kitty," the affectionate nickname everyone used when referring to her. She admired her elegance and charm, which sometimes had a touch of sadness to it.

It was the same with Senator Edward "Ted" Kennedy's wife, whom she admired very much. Like Liz, Joan Kennedy had been abandoned by her husband, and Liz, like many others, considered the senator's former wife to be a true Bostonian. She still lived in Boston and continued to attend and support many of the city's charitable affairs.

On the other hand, Liz had no use for Edward Kennedy. For her, the Chappaquiddick affair had proven his lack of class and character. In spite of his many positive achievements for Massachusetts, the senator belonged to a group of politicians who Liz felt could not be trusted because they had lied. In Kennedy's case, the events were clear and definite. They were less precise, however, for another Massachusetts politician to whom Liz allowed great leniency.

Representative Barney Frank's homosexual entanglements, which had been exploited in the Washington tabloids, should have led her to condemn him. But according to Liz, Frank had displayed a superior quality that should be required of all public figures—sincerity. And that was good enough for her.

In discussing the latest accusations in the press that demanded Barney Frank's resignation from Congress, Liz had convincingly replied: "I saw him on television last night. He tells the truth. He seems sincere. One can tell right away when someone is lying on television. He will not have to leave his position."

In spite of the cold and the humidity in the air, there were many people at Quincy Market when the three of us arrived shortly before noon. Fortunately there was not the glacial wind that hits you in the chest and that often blows through the waterfront docks.

I looked around, trying to give myself courage by thinking of something familiar I could hold onto. I looked up at the roof of Faneuil Hall for the famous weathervane in the shape of a huge grasshopper. I also thought about the American consuls who used the Faneuil Hall grasshopper as a code word during the War of 1812. But the weathervane had disappeared into the thick, grayish fog that obscured the entire marketplace.

Carved into huge ice blocks, and lined up side by side on the snow along Faneuil Hall's brick walls, were about twenty full-length Statues of Liberty, and another ten busts representing the Statue of Liberty's head. All the flashes from people taking photographs made the sculptures shine like large silver knives. The judges, who had already made their selections, stood on a small platform that was illuminated by harsh blinking lights. They were waiting to announce the winners and proceed with the distribution of prizes. It was now time for me to give my speech.

Because I wasn't satisfied with what I had written and was blinded by the flashes, I was a bit nervous as I walked up to the podium, rummaging through my overcoat pockets to find my speech and then through my jacket to find my glasses. I easily found my notes typed by Liz, but not my glasses. In our hasty departure and aggravated by Kenneth's unexpected presence, I hadn't checked that I had taken them as I usually do. I must have left them on my desk. I started to panic while trying to convince myself that I only needed to let go and be guided by inspiration. Liz was right. There was only God's help I could count on now. The committee chairperson had already announced my name; I must plunge in and take the microphone.

My comments about every human being's constant struggle to be free must have stirred the sentiment that not only Liz, but all Americans, value so highly—sincerity. I was vigorously applauded, especially by Kenneth and his mother, who were in the first row among the curious spectators eager to know the winners' names.

As part of his introduction, the announcer first commented about the French origins of both Peter Faneuil and Bartholdi. He then started to announce the winners and to distribute the lesser prizes: white T-shirts with a black silhouette of the Statue of Liberty's head. Finally, as the Bank of Boston's representative, I was asked to present the first prize: a plane ticket from Boston to Paris donated by Air France. The winner was a small, robust man dressed in a ski outfit who bounded up to the podium when he heard his name. He came from Maine, the land of ice sculptors. By its size alone, his work outshone all the others. His statue was three times larger than any other and must have been at least nine feet tall.

To thank me for participating in the prize distribution, the chairperson offered me a T-shirt.

When I found Liz and Kenneth shortly after, I was in a better mood, no doubt due to the positive turn of events. I invited them to have a hot choco-late at the Parker House Hotel. The hotel was not far from Faneuil Hall, and we could walk there. It was always a pleasure for me to sink into the cushy, warm atmosphere of the Parker House. The lights were dim, as they are in many of the hotel lobbies in the United States, but here the lighting leaned toward a darker red because of the reflection of the maple woodwork and the oriental rugs. There is a mysterious atmosphere here, perhaps left behind by John Wilkes Booth.

I asked Kenneth, "Did you know that John Wilkes Booth, a young actor from Boston, stayed at this very hotel before leaving to assassinate President Lincoln in a Washington theater?" Kenneth listened without saying anything; even though he was not shy, he didn't speak very much. It seemed that life had already taught him to keep quiet on many subjects. His mother was talkative, and he let her speak in his place.

"I saw the statue of Lincoln with the slaves," said Kenneth suddenly. "It's Mom who showed it to me when we went to see 'Les Misérables' at the Wang Center."

"Bravo!" I replied, while ruffling his hair. At a time when most young American boys had their hair almost shaved, his mother had left his rather long for someone his age. "Even if you're too young to know your country's history, you have a good memory!"

"Tell me, who cuts your hair?" He didn't answer and let his mother reply: "I know Luigi from church. He's the hairdresser at the beauty salon at the Ritz. When I bring Kenneth to his French classes at the French Library, once a month I take advantage of the time to stop at Luigi's. He cuts Kenneth's hair between customers."

It was then that I understood that Luigi did not charge anything for this service. Kenneth let her talk and smiled, showing his front teeth, very white and round, but, like his hair, a little bit long and too prominent.

"Liz, you should bring Kenneth to the dentist to have his front teeth aligned, especially the two middle ones; they're really like rabbit teeth."

"It's not worth the trouble," she replied. "They will soon fall out." Her response didn't seem very convincing to me. Had I forgotten that Liz was a proponent of Christian Science and she was unwavering in her convictions? I decided to change the subject: "And how is his French coming along?"

"I don't know if he will continue," she replied. "One class once a week is not enough to learn a language. But his father insists. He has already paid the full registration. He's never late with that because this is what he wants;

his school tuition is a whole different story. I'll need to ask the principal to telephone him."

"It would be a shame if Kenneth didn't learn French. You speak so well yourself; you could help him."

"Kenneth tells me that when he goes to his father's for vacation on Long Island, many of his father's friends speak French, and he doesn't understand anything. I don't think he will return to the French Library after vacation, and I don't know if Kenneth will return to his father's for vacation," continued Liz. "It's not a good environment for him."

"Yet you've told me that the judge gave your ex-husband the right to have his son during the summer months." I say this a bit dryly because I don't want to get into this discussion with Liz.

Through her comments, I realized that Liz's objections were about not doing what her former husband asked, that she was being stubborn, and above all, Kenneth should not come under his father's influence, even from a distance. Learning French was one of his ideas that must have had a hidden agenda.

I called the waiter to pay the bill, and I had no sooner put my credit card on the table than Liz turned toward the waiter and asked for a doggy bag. She wanted to take home the two croissants that she had not eaten, happy to merely drink her hot chocolate. "It will be for Kenneth's breakfast tomorrow morning," she mentioned in a very natural tone.

When we left the Parker House, it was starting to get dark. As we stepped out onto School Street, it was crowded with cars whose white headlights helped to effectively light up the pavement, street, and sidewalks. On the opposite side of the street, the windows of King's Chapel were lighted, most likely for a Saturday service that was taking place. A little farther, a bright sign shone on the untouched snow covering the courtyard in front of the building. The French restaurant Maison Robert was housed in a wing of the former Boston City Hall.

The three of us left heading in the direction of Tremont Street. Liz had decided to take the T with Kenneth at Park Street, and I was going to continue on foot, crossing the Common and the Public Garden to reach Commonwealth Avenue.

We walked along the snow-laden Old Granary Ground whose slate tombstones emerged from the fresh white powder and seemed to huddle around the granite obelisk dedicated to Benjamin Franklin's parents.

Once I reached the bottom of Park Street, I decided to return to Back Bay by going up Beacon Hill to the State House and not through the Common. I came into Commonwealth Avenue by taking Beacon Street and then Arlington. It was nighttime and it was wiser to avoid the Common, whose east side was next to the Combat Zone, the sketchy neighborhood in Boston known for drugs and prostitution.

Kenneth seemed to be tired of being outside as he stomped in the snow and mud. He complained of having cold feet. He wanted to go home. He wanted to watch television before going to bed. He wanted to be finally alone and quiet. He had made enough concessions to his mother, so now he felt he could tell her firmly that it was time to go home. I understood Kenneth and could empathize with what he was feeling. When I was his age, and when I had had enough, I would leave and take a walk in the fields that surrounded my house. Sometimes I would go all the way to the small woods, a bit far away from our home, which would worry my mother. The field's high grass would hide me, the trees' silence would overwhelm me, and the damp earth's pungent odor would intoxicate me—living in the city, Kenneth was not as fortunate.

I wanted to thank Liz and Kenneth for the time they devoted to me, for their lively companionship, for their enthusiastic applause at Quincy Market that had encouraged me, and for their sheer presence, which made me feel better. I decided to give Kenneth the T-shirt that the committee organizers had given me.

The white cotton top was not extraordinary, except that it was made for this special occasion and had the Statue of Liberty's tragic and crude black face on the front, which gave her a mystical allure that reminded me of the Shroud of Turin.

For me, it was a generous gesture because I like to keep the gifts that are often given to me at this type of event, not for their retail value but because they serve as a reminder when I feel a need to delve into my past. These tokens are useful to me. They aren't merely frills of the past but more like milestones or bookmarks; they define stages, events, dates, and meetings.

Maybe I wanted to make myself useful for something in Kenneth's life. Maybe I wanted to tell him that, first of all, he had to start by asserting his freedom, and it was better to do it now than later; a delayed revolt has more serious consequences affecting lives that are already established. A life should not be remade based on someone else's rubble. A life, if it has to be reinvented, must not be started over too late. I was relieved, as if I had finally found some meaning to the sorrowful face that seemed crowned with thorns on the T-shirt I had been given. This Statue of Liberty was lighting up the world. Finally, through pure vanity, maybe I wanted Kenneth to remember me someday in the future, and that would extend my life a bit.

"Kenneth, here, I'm giving you my T-shirt."

"But I already have one," replied Kenneth. "Mom asked if she could have one for me while we were waiting for you."

3

A FEAST OF KINGS

I had met many Franco-American couples since my arrival in Boston. They were almost always French women who had married American men. It was rarely the opposite.

The Franco-American couples I related to were already entering the third stage of their lives. They had met after the war and because of the war. Many American soldiers returned home with young French women they had met after the Normandy Landing.

Once these women had overcome the obstacles of their origins, when they had survived the difficulties of life and withstood the test of time, they retained something bigger from the events they had lived through. What made them different was a fragility that was very moving. That was the case with the Soares family.

Paul Soares met Madeleine Descouvres during the Liberation of Paris after the landing on the Normandy beaches. They were at a reception at City Hall organized by an association of young women, *les Marraines de Guerre de Paris*, who corresponded with soldiers. Paul later said that he had fallen in love with his future wife the moment she gave him a bouquet of flowers and whispered that she had nothing else to offer him. And her English was not bad at all. She had come from Antony, a Paris suburb where her parents lived and where she had picked the roses. Her parents had invited them for dinner the following Sunday.

Paul came from Massachusetts. He was born in Quincy, a suburb of Boston. His family came from Portugal and they were Jewish. His father arrived in New York before the First World War and after working as a foreman in a textile factory in Lowell, had established himself in Quincy, where he opened a clothing store. Paul, his only son, was 20 years old when the United States joined the war effort. He interrupted his studies, enlisted in the Navy, and a few days later left Boston on the SS Dorchester, which changed his life forever.

When he returned to the United States with Madeleine, Paul found a job as a comptroller with Jordan Marsh, a big department store on Washington Street in Boston. Madeleine worked there as a sales clerk before the birth of their two sons. At the end of the 1960s, Paul left Jordan Marsh to prepare for his Certified Public Accountant license exams, which he passed, and then opened his own business in the house they bought in Quincy. He still had an accounting business and lived with Madeleine in that same house, not far from his parents.

I met Madeleine first. She worked as a volunteer at the French Library in Boston, where she was in charge of sending out invitations to the many events the library organized all year long. Because she could draw well, they would ask her to make special decorations on the ones that went out at Christmas. Her designs, Gothic letters, and calligraphy in gold ink were quite impressive.

I had become a member of the French Library so I could read French newspapers and see some old French movies. The library had a significant Marcel Carné fund to use exclusively for events. A few days before Christmas I received an invitation that was written on two pages. The cover page was a reproduction of a nineteenth-century etching of children sledding on the Boston Common, but the border was hand painted with holly garlands intertwined with a red ribbon. On the second page was the invitation printed in English: General Georges F. Doriot, President of the French

Library, invited me to attend a concert followed by a reception. My name was written in Gothic letters penned in gold ink. I was charmed by this elegant, slightly old-fashioned card that evoked a Christmas tale in Boston.

When I arrived at the concert, the acting director, Mrs. Cathy Joyce, was greeting guests since General Doriot was ill that evening. I told her how much I liked the beautiful invitation I had received. After the concert, just when I was about to leave, I saw Mrs. Joyce coming toward me leading an older woman by the arm. She said, "Monsieur, before you leave, let me introduce you to Mrs. Soares. She's the one who designed the invitation you admired so much. Madeleine is part of our volunteer group. Without our volunteers, without our benefactors, we would not be able to function."

I exchanged a few words with Madeleine, merely asking her if she was French. I did have time to notice her timid look, a bit lost behind her large framed glasses. I sensed she was moved by my compliments about her work, and it seemed to mean a lot to her.

Shortly afterward, I received another invitation that immediately reminded me of the one I had received from the French Library. Right away, I recognized Madeleine's handwriting on the envelope as well as her brush strokes on the invitation. But this time the invitation was even brighter, and the design was painted with real gouache. It showed the Magi traveling to Bethlehem under a starry night. Their robes were dazzling, and one of them was so ornate it seemed to embody all of Africa. On the reverse side, the invitation was written entirely by hand, always in Gothic letters but different from the previous invitation; this one was written in French and with black ink: M et Mme Paul Soares were inviting me to Quincy for *la fête des rois*.

I would be able to accept their invitation because the Epiphany was celebrated on Sunday, a day I didn't work. The taxi driver who agreed to drive me there started to grumble; he didn't like to go to an area he didn't know well, unsure if he would find a client for the ride back. In this deserted suburb that was disappearing under the snow, it took him awhile to find the street where Paul and Madeleine lived. After several mistakes he stopped in front of an open drugstore and got out to get directions. Wanting to thank him for his thoughtful initiative and knowing he was from Haiti, when he returned, I spontaneously started talking to him in French. That was enough to put him in a good mood.

Their house was on the outskirts of Quincy, on the ocean side of the Southern Artery, on a quiet street lined with small houses that were all alike.

Paul greeted me, smiling and obviously happy that he too was able to speak French. He led me into the living room and introduced me to the other guests: a middle-aged couple and their daughter.

The corner of the living room reserved for sitting was not very spacious. It contained an assortment of furniture, easy chairs, sideboards, and tables in light oak, sycamore style, square and big like those manufactured during the post-war years. The sitting area was arranged around a big, old-fashioned television set. The large chairs with wooden armrests facing the television were so crowded together that I had a hard time moving in to greet the guests who had arrived before me. They seemed older than the Soareses. Their daughter had a round face and curly hair and seemed younger than she was. All three got up together and greeted me in French. They were all the same size, small in stature and neatly dressed.

Introducing them, Paul said, "This is George Shay and his wife, Jeanne, who is French like Madeleine. Like us, they met in Paris during the Liberation, and Suzy, their daughter, who works at Fidelity, an investment firm in the Prudential Center."

Paul showed me to my place between Mr. and Mrs. Shay. I sat down and as the conversation started, Mr. Shay said, "We met Paul and Madeleine here in Quincy. Our houses are a few blocks away from each other, and since our wives were French, we got along right away."

Mrs. Shay interrupted: "You know, I am still French even though I left France right after the war. I still have my French passport, I am still registered at the Consulate, but I don't vote anymore. I voted just up to De Gaulle. Everything was clear with De Gaulle, but now I don't understand anything."

"We still go to France every two to three years," added Mr. Shay. "I always like to go back to Paris even though many things have changed. We don't eat as well as before. There has been a lot of construction. My wife's parents had a furniture store on the boulevard Diderot in the 12th arrondissement. I met Jeanne on July 14, 1945, at a dance that the firemen held at their station on the rue de Chaligny. I had gone with a Frenchman who lived in the neighborhood and who was also a soldier. My in-laws' store has been gone for a long time, but the fire station with its castle-like tiny towers is still there."

Madeleine came out of the kitchen, which was next to the living room. The wall separating the kitchen from the eating area had an opening through which meals are passed. Madeleine had made a lot of noise opening it when I arrived and gave me a warm *Bonjour* as though she were on stage. She must have spent some time carefully choosing the black dress and small red apron with white flowers she wore to serve dinner. Her hairdo was meticulous, exactly like Mrs. Shay's. They most likely spent the previous day at the same hairdresser for a color and perm, but Madeleine had tied her hair back with a large imitation strass gem barrette, and her glasses with the extra-large frames made her appear more American than Mrs. Shay.

After affectionately kissing all her guests on both cheeks in the French manner, Madeleine announced, as any great chef would, "Hurry to finish your aperitifs. We must be seated or dinner will be burned."

Madeleine had indicated I should be seated to her right, and as I was sitting down at the table, I noticed that the walls in this part of the room, serving as a dining area, were covered with paintings, all a large format and not framed. It was obvious that all these paintings had been created by the same artist: they were all in maroons, browns, and blacks. It was as if the canvases were black shrouds that had been slashed with a large knife. Their abstract nature jarred with the décor of the house; they were in sharp contrast with the furniture. They seemed almost out of place with the many objects and photographs in a variety of frames that crammed the shelves above the sideboards and against the walls.

In an attempt to please my hosts, to compliment them on their good taste, at least concerning this aspect of their décor, I said, "I like your paintings a lot." I was exaggerating a bit, but I was also sincere because I was struck by an element of desperation and violence that emanated from them, a sort of cry. An awkward silence followed my compliments, and I noticed a vacant look in Madeleine's eyes, one I had noticed before when I first met her at the French Library.

"Our oldest son, Jack, painted them," said Paul, then immediately added, "Madeleine spent the entire morning in the kitchen. We must savor her meal; she's a true French cook."

On the table, laden with plates, place settings, and glasses, each guest had three different-colored glasses, fine and shiny as if they had just come from the Sandwich Glass Company. Madeleine had put out silver candlesticks and small porcelain boxes. She had strewn some small holly branches here and there on what was left of the white tablecloth. A menu she had designed and painted was next to each guest.

At the top of the menu a white card displayed my first name written in Gothic letters and gold ink. It blended in among tiny stars that had been individually cut from gold paper and glued to the menu to remind us that we were celebrating the Epiphany. A shield was painted at a left angle. I recognized three blue lilies above a Phrygian cap painted red with a tricolor rosette and the French coat of arms. Still at the top of the menu, and now at a right angle, a stream of green water poured from a tilted vase, the symbol of Aquarius, my astrological sign. I thought Madeleine must have seen my birth date on my French Library registration form. Even if the illustration on the menu was a little childish, the technique was strong and revealed a real talent. In bright letters, she had also listed the courses, a truly royal lunch: a soufflé, Maine lobster, a leg of lamb, French cheeses, the Kings' cake, and Mumm Champagne. The soufflé was delicious. Everyone had seconds. Then Madeleine asked Paul to go carve the lamb in the kitchen.

"But I thought there was another course before the lamb," Paul said softly in Madeleine's direction.

"Oh, yes, that's right," she responded. "But I completely forgot and left the lobsters in the freezer. Since I wrote the menu yesterday, I didn't want to start all over again."

Mrs. Shay added, "Madeleine, your meal is already very copious. We can do without it, and I want to save some room for the cake."

I hurried to say something to change the conversation: "Madeleine, your drawings are magnificent. I think you must have spent a lot of time doing all those invitations for the French Library and then all the menus for today's lunch. They are truly very well done. I am sure General Doriot appreciates your work and likes your style that depicts the Christmas season so well. He himself paints lovely bouquets, a bit like the samurai who painted on fans once the war was over."

"I don't know," said Madeleine. "I started working with his wife, Edna, who is American. She liked what I did. In any case, it keeps me occupied. You know, I took art lessons; I was in my first year at Le Musée des Arts Decoratifs when I met Paul. I wanted to be a decorator, a window dresser. I gave up everything to come here."

Paul let his wife talk. It seemed he did not want to say anything to contradict her. On the contrary, he tried to help her by supporting what she was saying. "The first years were difficult," he said, nodding. "And when the two boys were born, Madeleine stayed home to take care of them. She didn't start painting again until much later."

All of a sudden Madeleine seemed to become more talkative. "We always lived in Quincy, but not in this house," she continued. "At the beginning, when we arrived from France, we rented a small wooden house closer to the ocean. I liked it a lot there, and so did the children. We could walk along the beach. Jack liked to go to the beach; he would go very far, all alone, even in winter. Mark preferred to stay home and play with his Erector set. Then we bought this house next to Paul's parents in 1960. It was bigger, and each boy could have his own bedroom. That's when we met the Shays, who were our neighbors. And we became friends right away."

"Madeleine, do you remember when you arrived with Paul, who was driving a truck loaded with all your furniture?" asked Mr. Shay. "Jeanne and I wanted to help, but when you discovered that Jeanne was French, the two of you never stopped talking. You didn't even help us to unload the truck."

Madeleine laughed and continued: "A few years ago when the boys left for college, I started painting again to help pay their expenses. I had read an ad in the newspaper announcing a position for an esthetician to promote beauty products, and you could work in your own home. I lied a little, but since I knew colors very well, I was hired. I set up a small beauty salon in Jack's room. The company that hired me, Hollywood Cosmetics, provided a special bed that tilted, and two or three shelves where I was to display all types of jars, samples, and tubes of cream. Jack was furious when he came home. He couldn't find any of his things. It was a lot of work for very little pay, especially when it started to get warm. I had to buy a small refrigerator for the products because they would melt and I couldn't use them. My job was to clean the client's skin, apply makeup, and especially try to sell them the products afterward. I was also supposed to advise my clients on the choice of colors for their clothing. The company had given me a book, which I memorized; it gave answers according to the color of eyes and hair, and skin tone. I was to sell shampoos, hair colorings, and sprays also. It became very expensive for the clients so they never returned. At the end of one year I stopped. Paul thought it was not profitable. I miss it a bit because I liked to chat with the clients. They told me about their lives."

Perhaps because she wanted to be gentle with Madeleine, Suzy added, "You were too easy, Madeleine. You were giving free makeup sessions to all the neighbors. You did mine for me when I was graduating from Brandeis."

"You did wonderful work," interrupted Mrs. Shay. "Poor Suzy, who was so pale because she had spent months indoors preparing for her exams. It was difficult for you to put makeup on a young girl, but with two or three strokes of your brush you put some color into her cheeks and made her healthy again!"

"But there were others who weren't happy!" said Madeleine, bursting out laughing. "One day a man insulted me on the telephone. He had given his wife a certificate for a makeup session and color consultation for her birthday and when she got home, she started to take all her clothes out of the closet and hold them up to the light in the window. The colors did not match those I had advised for her. Fortunately, these folks were not from Quincy. They lived in Hingham and had a lot of money."

Paul passed the plates, cleared the table, and served the champagne, all while glancing back at Madeleine. We couldn't detect the slightest amount of disapproval, even when Madeleine repeated that, to come all the way here, she had abandoned everything: Paris that she adored, a well-off family, a job as a window dresser, a career as a decorator or maybe an artist. But Paul did not seem to reproach any of his wife's comments. Madeleine was recalling facts she had accepted and that were in the past. Didn't she and Paul know, deep inside, that their meeting had led them to a life that transcended the ordinary?

I dared not mention their sons. I sensed it was better to avoid the subject. But Madeleine, who hadn't moved from her chair for quite a while, reminded us of the visible and invisible presence of Jack and the absence of his brother. "Jack takes after me," she said suddenly while pointing to the canvases that covered the walls in the dining area. "He's the one who did all these paintings. There are even more in his room. He painted them when he was a student in New York and studying at the School of Fine Arts." Then, after gazing at them a while she added, "His brother doesn't like them. Mark was supposed to come to Quincy for the holidays. He should have been here today, but he had to work and couldn't come."

"That's true," said Suzy. "I called him to wish him a Happy New Year, and he told me he had some projects he needed to work on for the mayor's office. You know, it's great that he was chosen as one of the architects to help renovate Copley Place. Mark's going to be a great Boston architect someday."

The conversation stopped for a moment, each person remaining silent. I asked myself what could have happened to Jack, whose life since childhood appeared so unique. Mark's attitude was more straightforward. He was a son who wanted to succeed and who worked hard. It was Madeleine who broke the silence. Getting up from the table and going toward the kitchen, she said, "This time I mustn't forget the dessert, I must not forget the cake. I have to reheat it, but I must warn you right away, I'm not the one who made it. With all the invitations I had to send out for the French Library, I didn't have time. I bought it from the new baker who just opened a place in Back Bay on Arlington Street. They say he is French. His store is called Paris Bakery. It's right next to the Unitarian Church. I think it will be good."

As luck would have it, my slice of the traditional cake had the bean. I would be the king, and as my queen, I selected Madeleine, who seemed to think this choice was perfectly natural. She was radiant, but lost in her memories, in her dreams.

When it was time to leave, Mrs. Shay offered to drive me to the T that was closest to their house. "I'll drive you all the way to Quincy Adams, which is on the Red Line. Once in Boston, you only have to get off at Park Street. That will be more reliable and much less expensive than a taxi." Suzy offered to drive me instead, but her mother insisted and had already put on her coat and boots.

Outside a fine, cold drizzle was falling and it was dark. Quincy was peaceful. We quickly reached the center of town, empty and quiet at the end of the weekend. The Church of the Presidents dominated the square, disdainfully reminding this suburban working-class neighborhood of its lofty origins.

Mrs. Shay drove her big car calmly and skillfully. Without saying anything she stopped in front of the T station.

"You know," she told me briskly, "Madeleine was very happy that you were able to come to their home for *la fête des rois*. She was afraid that you wouldn't be able to accept."

"But no, I wanted to come."

As usual, I was looking to diminish the scope of my gesture. I had come not only for Madeleine but also to occupy my Sunday; one is never completely generous. I said, "It was easy for me. The invitation was for a Sunday."

Mrs. Shay added, "Madeleine has suffered a lot. She has never recovered, never completely recovered after Jack's death. When he committed suicide in New York, she was extremely distraught. Fortunately, Paul was there for her."

Just before I got out of the car, as though she wanted to tell me something very important, Mrs. Shay said, "I hope you'll come back to Quincy soon. Madeleine told me you remind her so much of Jack."

4

HARVARD SQUARE

In the album *'Round About Midnight* by Miles Davis, I am always eager to hear "All of You," the number that comes right after "'Round Midnight," and "Ah-Leu-Cha." Maybe it's because I find it a little less scary than the first two numbers. Maybe it's because that was the tune we were listening to in the car one Saturday night in January when Joe and I were driving to Cambridge to pick up the Sunday edition of the *Boston Globe*.

"You know," Joe was saying, "I already know you quite well. You're cold, stubborn, and very few things make you happy."

On Saturday night after dinner, I was in the habit of going to meet Joe at his condominium in Bay Village. Because I wanted to get some exercise after a week spent in the office, I would walk from Commonwealth Avenue to his home. Each time I was pleased to see the small doll-like houses of Bay Village at the corner of Fayette Street, as if I were seeing them for the first time. They were so close to one another, as if they wanted to protect themselves from the harsh times and to hide their history, like people avoiding an unpleasant gathering or hiding an ugly birthmark.

I liked to linger in Joe's apartment. The paintings and engravings were hung to form a grid on the walls, and I liked to stop there for a moment in peace and quiet, taking advantage of the mild temperature of the rooms.

Joe was adamant that the thermostat for the radiators remain at 75 degrees Fahrenheit all winter long. In Boston, this was a luxury that could only be indulged in by a foreigner. Joe was Italian and worked at the bank as I did.

I had fun making him plead with me to leave the apartment to go to Cambridge. "Why do we have to go?" I'd say. "We are so comfortable here. You have the best heated house in Boston!"

My remarks hit home every time. Joe didn't reply but immediately put on his overcoat while quickly admiring the collection of engravings devoted to the robbers of Naples and Sicily that he had accumulated over many years; he gazed at them as if they were gold. It was as though he wanted to make sure I understood there were more interesting things in his apartment than the heating.

Without looking at Joe, who was getting impatient, and while I was having difficulty getting out of my armchair, I added: "Since you're completely myopic, I don't think it's wise to go all the way to Cambridge with you." I was hardly exaggerating. On certain nights such as this, when it was raining so hard in Boston, it was a veritable feat to go from Bay Village to Harvard Square where the newspaper kiosk remained open all night.

All the one-way streets that lead to the Expressway, and Storrow Drive along the Charles River, are enough to drive you crazy. On Storrow Drive you have to have steady nerves and a lot of courage to squeeze between the speeding cars with their glaring headlights. You must also be alert as you pass the buildings housing the Harvard libraries, which, like the newspaper kiosk, are open all night and lighted until dawn. They're like a beacon so that you don't miss the Anderson Bridge exit, the bridge that finally brings you right to the middle of Harvard Square.

Actually, Joe knew the route very well. He had taken it many times to go to the cemetery after the death of his American wife. It was she who had encouraged him to apply for a position at the Bank of Boston. He knew the good shortcuts and weaved easily between the cars. He drove like a robot, but a robot with Italian resources, his nose low to the steering wheel, his eyes going from the windshield to the rearview mirror and back, always staying to the right without noticing that he was splashing large jets of water on our windows.

Once at Harvard Square, Joe didn't park the car but stopped along the sidewalk as close as possible to the kiosk. He often double-parked to let me off to get the voluminous edition of the *Boston Sunday Globe* that had just arrived. I would buy two copies; then I would grab the two large bulky packages of paper. In spite of their thickness, I was able to protect one as well as I could under my raincoat; this one would be Joe's, as he hated to have his newspaper soaked with water. I used mine to cover my head briefly to get back to the car without getting too wet.

Joe opened the door for me and, this time, with a big grin on his face said, "You're wonderful."

Before heading back to Boston, Joe would take the time to light a cigarette and take only a few puffs. Then he would throw the whole cigarette, still burning, out the window, before diligently and silently concentrating again on his driving. He didn't go back by Storrow Drive but went down Broadway, less traveled than the Expressway. It divides Cambridge in two, the west from the east, and crosses an area of abandoned industrial buildings lining the highway up to the Longfellow Bridge. From there, he would go downtown by Charles Street.

Knowing that it would please me, and to show he was grateful for my friendship and for getting the newspapers, Joe put the Miles Davis cassette back in the tape deck. I was already moved by the clarity of the first notes the quintet played, and following the troubling sounds of "'Round Midnight" and "Ah-Leu-Cha" came the more reassuring and tender melody of "All of You." But I was left with a sensation that life is bittersweet.

After all, I thought to myself, you only need a few things to make you happy.

5

LOWELL–KEROUAC

M ike worked at the Shawmut Bank. I had met him during a campaign that was competing with my bank, the Bank of Boston. He couldn't understand why I liked Lowell, the site of a close-knit French Canadian community known as the "Francos" and the birthplace of Jack Kerouac, considered the father of the "Beat" generation. The sad and shabby appearance of the city repelled Mike. He was astounded that I could talk about it with such emotion.

I told him that Lowell was one of a small number of cities that have a mystery—a hidden sense about them that is not apparent right away—and that you are drawn to them precisely for that reason. He responded that he preferred to live in a city that was "clean and safe" and where you could find pleasure from going "shopping." Although he had been to Lowell many times for work, he never thought of visiting the neighborhoods where the old warehouses and closed factories were or even venturing toward the canals.

Mike had never read a single line of Kerouac's writings. He knew nothing about him or the "beatniks." As for the Francos, he thought he might have met some without realizing who they were. He remembered that at Merrimack College, a Catholic University in Massachusetts where he had studied, many of his classmates had French names, but not one of them could speak French. There were also two or three priests who came from Montreal who spoke with a funny accent, but they were forbidden to speak French by the university.

As a tribute to Kerouac (born Jean-Louis Kerouac in 1922), the city of Lowell decided to dedicate this year to him. They planned to establish a park, which was really just a small square planted with a few trees. They also organized several events, including tonight's conference with Beat generation poets Allen Ginsberg and Gregory Corso. I invited Mike to come with me and to leave Boston early so, before going to the event, I could show him what I liked about Lowell.

As often happens in New England during the month of January, all the suburbs of Boston were covered with fresh snow. The scenery reminded me of clean, fresh, spotless, satin sheets. The light of day was so pure that the snowy landscape looked like an etching. More frequently than we care to admit, these days are followed by truly glacial nights, which are equally clear and transparent. Often, when coming back from Lowell in this same kind of weather late at night, I noticed that high above the quiet, silent countryside there were many stars in the sky. They seemed so close it was as if they were guiding my way.

Though Lowell is only about thirty miles from Boston, it seems farther, probably because you have to drive through an area of valleys and some woods to get there. Upon leaving Boston, for a while you follow Route 128, the high-tech highway, through heavy traffic until suddenly reaching Route 3, a much narrower and provincial road. Halfway there, we cross over the Concord River where it joins the Merrimack River in Lowell—the river of the Indians, the Canuts, and the river of Kerouac. Ever since my youth in the Creuse region of France, I have always believed there were some rivers and streams that are destined to serve mankind by providing work and, more important, providing the comfort and solace that softens torment and troubles. The Merrimack River was one of these.

I was happy to return to Lowell on this winter night. I had viewed a video entitled *What Happened to Kerouac* many times, so I was thrilled to be able to meet some of Kerouac's friends, who had become familiar to me. A friend from Harvard, who had loaned me the video, was another one who couldn't understand why I would devote such admiration to a character who, according to him, was so unlike me. I had read almost all of Kerouac's works that had been translated into French. I had also read his biography in English by Ann Charters and Allen Ginsberg's journal published several years ago in Paris.

I took Mike to the places Kerouac had lived. I retraced the route I had taken during my first visit there with Father Morissette, a Franco priest from Lowell, who had been close to Kerouac during his youth, and to whom I had written. In my letter I told him of my passion for Kerouac's work and even more of my joy and astonishment at being sent to Boston, so close to Lowell. Later, I took this tour many times with Roger Brunelle, Red Ouellette, and other Francos from Lowell who had known Jack, as they preferred to call him.

I wanted to start Mike's tour at the end of Kerouac's story, perhaps because it would answer many questions and shed light on his life. First, we went to Saint Jean Baptiste Church. The Francos had built it themselves and with such fury. It was as if they wanted to establish their own cathedral on American soil. Kerouac was buried from Saint Jean Baptiste Church, and it was Father Morissette who said the mass. Unlike many Francos, Father Morissette had a true affection for Kerouac, which allowed him to understand and forgive everything about him.

Seen from the outside, the church seemed very tall, perched at the top of many steps. The inside, an immense nave with pseudo-gothic arches, appeared large and empty. The side altars were stripped bare, with only a few statues. The main altar, noble and austere, would suit the Jansenists. Because of its gray color, I wondered if it was built of granite, but it was really constructed with brick. It reminded me of some churches in Brittany.

To see the church so empty, even on Sundays, saddened Father Morissette. "Between the two wars the church was always full. People stopped going to church at the beginning of the 1960s when the factories shut down and people had to look for work far from the center of town." Father Morissette kept repeating that the masses were magnificent up until then. "Before leaving for New York," he continued, "Jack would come here with his parents. He was always well dressed. Even later, when he returned to Lowell, he wouldn't want to be seen in his Beat clothes; his mother wouldn't have liked that either, besides, it wasn't characteristic of him."

Making a good impression seemed important to Father Morissette. In his case, his clerical suit was always freshly pressed and his white collar properly starched. His shoes were not like those usually worn by other priests. They were quality laced shoes, and you could tell they came from a well-known store. There is a rumor that at a certain age he decided to wear a wig. He was pleased with the results provided by the reputable wig maker he had chosen. The hair, more gray than black, was thick and intermingled with white strands. It was the side part, which appeared to be too straight, and the little white tufts protruding at the neck that were the only indications his coif was not real.

The story goes that during World War II, when he had to greet French ships pulling into the port of Boston, his concern for being well dressed led him to wear a uniform resembling that of a naval officer, except it had a roman collar without decorations. However, it would not be his appearance but his service to the French navy that would later earn him entry into the Legion of Honor. In fact, because he spoke French fluently, like all the Francos of his generation, he had been named Chaplin of the French Warships making a stop-over in Boston.

During the war, Father Morissette boarded the French ships to say mass, give sermons, hear confessions, and visit the sick. He also served as a moderator and untangled many unpleasant issues between the police and customs officers.

He would arrange for the French sailors, mostly from Brittany, to visit Franco families on Sundays so they would have a good meal and a pleasant outing. And at Christmas he would ask the France Forever Committee of Lowell women to prepare packages of books and sweets for them.

One day I asked Father Morissette: "What was your impression of Kerouac in 1966 when he returned to Lowell after being gone since 1939? Did you think he had changed after such a long separation? He had just finished an important work, the accomplishment of a lifetime. He had become famous, and not only in America."

The priest replied: "He was the same boy that I had known. He had kept his faith. He liked to drink. He was good to his mother, and he was good to his wife. He would come to Saint Jean Baptiste often. He liked to linger at the Grotto of Lourdes. Jack could easily have lost himself when he went to New York. He was only seventeen years old. His mother advised him to go to Columbia instead of Boston College where he had received a football scholarship. I think she was right. At Boston College he would not have had the experiences that he received at Columbia, being in contact with all kinds of people he would never have met in Lowell, and people he would not have met at a Catholic college."

I wanted to show Mike the Archambault Funeral Home on Pawtucket Street where Kerouac was waked before his funeral at Saint Jean Baptiste. For several generations the same Franco family had owned this funeral home. I was familiar with the funeral home, since I had attended a wake for Paul Blanchette, who had died in an accident in the Alps. It had happened shortly after he had retired while taking his first trip to France in the hope of finding his ancestral roots. There were lots of people in the Archambault viewing rooms that night. It was very hot in spite of the large air conditioners in the windows. There was a group of Francos just in front of me, and I could hear them whispering in French; the Francos spoke French only among themselves.

Our next stop, Lupine Road, where Kerouac spent his childhood, is just outside the city on a small wooded hillside in a quiet neighborhood. His house, where his parents rented only one floor, was made of wood, painted white and, if my memory serves me well, had a covered balcony, more like a type of porch. As was the custom here, all the windows were closed. This made the house look mysterious and secretive, made more so by the shadows reflected by the early dusk slowly enveloping the hillside. For a while Mike and I walked around the house to see it from a distance. The sidewalks were swept only in a few places. Large piles of dirty frozen snow blocked the street. At this hour, the street was empty; the people who lived here had not come home from work yet.

Mike said, "This house is like the house where I was born, in Hull, south of Boston. It's a house for poor people, but in Hull I had the ocean. Every day I would go running on the beach, which was several miles long. Sometimes I'd play the trumpet as loud as I could; I didn't bother anyone, and no one came to listen to me. Kerouac only had this street where he could lose himself."

"You're right," I replied. "Kerouac liked to play in the street. When his mother went back to work making shoes, he spent long days outdoors. He would go to play along the Merrimack River, which in Lowell is like a street bordered by factories and towered over by giant red chimneys." Suddenly I saw the parallels in our lives. "Mike, you had the ocean. He had the river, and I had the staircase. For my sister and me, it was a staircase five stories high in a Parisian building. Because there wasn't an elevator, my mother wasn't worried, and she would let us play there."

I suggested to Mike that we drive around Pawtucketville before going to the lecture that was scheduled for six o'clock. It was a Franco neighborhood where the Kerouacs had lived for a while. Because the Kerouacs had moved so often and the street names changed, we got a bit lost, and we were late arriving at the movie theatre where the ceremony was being held. The auditorium was filled; there were many university students. Father Morissette had saved us two places in the middle of a row occupied by Francos. Among them were the leaders of Franco organizations and associations, not only in Lowell but in Manchester, New Hampshire, and other cities in Massachusetts, Rhode Island, and Maine.

Father Morissette introduced us to Eugene Lemieux and Réal Gilbert from *Saint John the Baptist Union of Manchester*, Claire Quintal of Assumption

College, and Paul Cotté of the *Journal de Lowell*. I wondered if the presence of these Francos meant the community had accepted the unorthodox author as one of their own. Kerouac was well liked in Quebec. Could his popularity there have influenced the New England Francos? Could they overcome their unwillingness to accept the success of one of their own who had strayed from their rigid morality? The Francos are different from the Quebecois; they are more reserved, more secretive, and more scrupulous. Maybe this is because they suffered more—by virtue of British colonization and American capitalism. But, like their brothers from Quebec, the New England Francos are very proud of their French ancestry and the role they played in the industrial development of the American Northeast. Nearly twenty years after the death of Jack Kerouac, were the Francos finally reconciled to accepting and honoring their most illustrious native son?

The program seemed long to me. I had difficulty following the English in the poems and certain passages taken from Kerouac's different works. Allen Ginsberg read many and was accompanied by a guitar. Gregory Corso appeared very emotional; he could barely recite two or three poems in spite of gulping at a bottle of whiskey. Most speakers were from the University of Lowell.

Exiting the theatre, I noticed Mike had a pack of books under his arm. He said, "During intermission, while you were talking with your Franco friends, I went to the stand down the hall where they were selling some of Kerouac's books and also some papers written about his life."

I was curious to know what he selected. "I took The Town and The City because of our tour of Lowell today. And I also took the biography of Kerouac written by Charles Jarvis because the salesperson recommended it. I took some brochures about the small park and the monument that will be dedicated to Kerouac in June. You'll like the monument; it reminds me of those tall stone pillars erected in prehistoric times in Western Europe, the Breton menhirs."

Later, when I asked Mike if he had read the books he had bought that night, he told me that he had started by reading the biography by Charles

Jarvis, and then he had read one after the other, *Doctor Sax*, and *On the Road*. He only read *The Town and the City* after the other two—a long time after—and of the three it was the last one that he liked best.

When I asked him what he liked about Kerouac, Mike hesitated a little before answering: "Just like Kerouac, I belong to an ethnic group that had trouble establishing itself in the Boston area. My family is Irish, and, even though the Irish integrated themselves without too much difficulty, I can understand all the injustices and humiliation the people from Quebec were subjected to and why Kerouac sought to escape this society that made him and them outcasts."

I pointed out that, even though they were Catholic, the Irish hardly supported the French Canadians, at least according to Mrs. Biron-Peloquin of the Franco-American Historical Society. Her father owned *L'Etoile*, the Franco newspaper in Lowell. Because the Francos were hard workers, conscientious, and were sought after by American bosses, the Irish workers in Boston forbade them access to the city for fear the Francos would take their jobs, she said. The Irish were savagely aggressive toward them; their fights were extremely violent—sometimes drawing blood.

Mike confided that there were other reasons he felt close to Kerouac. "I needed sun and warmth when I left Boston for Saint Croix and the other Caribbean islands. I think I visited them all. I don't like the winter and snow as much as you do. I needed to be free, and like Kerouac, all that sun, alcohol, and drugs messed with my brain. And I too ended up coming home, and I started to adjust; the beginning was difficult, but I met a lot of people like me. I haven't had a drink of alcohol for three years now." Laughingly, Mike finished his confession by saying: "And furthermore, I believe that I also remained faithful to the Grotto of Lourdes without even making a detour to Buddhism." Mike had well interpreted Kerouac's works.

While leaving the theatre to go back to the car, I said to Mike, "I think this honor to Kerouac would be incomplete if we didn't go to the cemetery to pay tribute to him before heading back to Boston." My suggestion didn't surprise him. We had begun our tour at the end, and we had to finish at the end. Mike was quick to reply, "I have a flashlight in the trunk." I automatically took the driver's seat and Mike sat next to me without saying a word.

I drove toward the Edson Catholic Cemetery, located outside the city. I thought I could find Jack Kerouac's burial plot, but there was neither a monument nor a tombstone. A flat slab placed on the dirt marked his place. Stella Sampas, his wife, who is now by his side, no doubt didn't want it any other way. The doors to the cemetery were closed. We climbed over the small wall of the gate. Because the cemetery was entirely covered with snow, it almost looked like daylight. The flashlight was useless. I could remember quite well the section of the cemetery where Kerouac was buried, but I couldn't find it. The snow made the search impossible. It had leveled the mounds of dirt, erasing the names on the inscriptions.

I remembered seeing an old video: In it, Father Morissette is there, right in the middle of the snow-covered cemetery. He is walking down a path. He is going toward a grave. He is kneeling next to it. He is contemplating, as though he is praying, respectful, as if in the presence of someone important who has earned a glorious place in eternity. Then, in the same gentle manner as he would wipe the face of the child who had come to him on such a winter day many years before, he slowly brushes the snow covering the stone's inscription of Ti Jean—or "Little John," as his Franco mother affectionately called him as a child—and the dates of his earthly adventure emerge.

"Ti Jean"
John L. KEROUAC
March 12, 1922–Oct. 21, 1969
He honored life
Stella his wife
Nov. 11, 1918–

As it was for Father Morissette in the video, it is this recollection of Kerouac as a child and young man, a good son, a good Christian, a good Franco, an avid football player that dominates my memory. Shouldn't it erase the one of the immoral Kerouac of the Beat generation and all that implies? Shouldn't the two have co-existed? Shouldn't they have been super-imposed one onto the other, mixed to create only one and not be separated, because they were both the same unique person?

Several months later, on a Saturday near the end of June at the dedication of the small park in Lowell, there were quite a few survivors who had shared Kerouac's Beat lifestyle. Allen Ginsberg was there of course. Also, Lawrence Ferlinghetti, who promised to send me some poems Kerouac wrote in French, and Gerald Nicosia, author of the memorable *Memory Babe: A Critical Biography of Jack Kerouac*. Sitting among them was Stella Sampas, Kerouac's wife, straight and dignified, her purse on her knees and her hands one over the other. She listened and said nothing. I wondered if she had been the one who wanted this city to be Jack's permanent resting place. Born and raised in Lowell, she knew better than anyone else the hidden and special meaning that Lowell had for Jack Kerouac: the city of his roots.

I went back to the Edson Catholic Cemetery on that humid day in June. A warm, brisk wind was blowing the dust in the alleys and the growth on the trees. I approached the grave. It was only a small square of earth covered with a stone marker, small bits of paper blown about, empty bottles and crushed beer cans littered the ground.

Let winter return! Let the snow return! Let us celebrate this child of winter!

6

ISABELLA STEWART
GARDNER MUSEUM

A nthony and Carla were members of one of the many small chamber orchestras in New England. Anthony, who went by Tony, was a pianist and Carla was a cellist. They were originally from Boston and had studied at the Boston Conservatory at the same time. They married shortly after graduating and had been married for ten years. They lived in a pretty little apartment on the Fenway right next to the Isabella Stewart Gardner Museum, and this winter they were lucky to have a contract to perform in the Tuesday evening concerts at the museum.

They seemed happy.

I met them in September shortly after my arrival in Boston. A mutual friend, Joel Cohen, the director of the Boston Camerata, introduced us.

Tony had a generous air about him, and Carla's appearance had something mysterious, which appealed to me. Up until now, the end of January, I had rarely missed their Tuesday concerts.

My office at the Bank of Boston was on Clarendon Street. To get to the museum before six o'clock, I'd leave in a hurry and ride the T instead of taking my car. From the Green Line I'd get off at the Ruggles stop on

Huntington Avenue. I'd finally arrive at the Isabella Stewart Gardner Museum after running in rain or snow, so common on these wintry days. The last time I saw them, Tony had said to me, "We are having some friends over for dinner after the concert next Tuesday. Please join us."

I knew that Tony and Carla had difficulty making ends meet, and they lived partly off an allowance from Tony's family. Tony had multiple gigs; he played the organ in churches and the piano in hotels. This year he was accompanying the weekly silent films at the French Library for their program, "Les Pionniers du Cinéma." He also gave piano lessons, which he taught at his students' homes so as not to disturb Carla. During his remaining free time, he wrote music—in other words, he composed almost nothing.

That night, when I came out of the subway on Huntington Avenue, the rain was falling in buckets, the sidewalks were like streams, and the cars splashed large sprays of water as they sped by on the sunken pavement.

The concert lovers, however, had not been discouraged by the rain. A large crowd had gathered in the stairway of the museum and was moving toward the big Tapestry Room, where the concert would take place. Neither rain nor snow will prevent Bostonians from attending a show or a musical event. Perhaps only a hurricane would hold them back!

Tony had left my ticket at the box office. After getting it, I knew I'd have to squeeze my way toward the cloakroom and take my place among those who were checking their umbrellas, hats, and coats. Besides, they all take their time to remove the precious and indispensable rubbers covering their shoes, which they would carefully put in plastic bags, then cautiously and politely hand them to the coat check attendants.

Reaching the second floor, I found the Tapestry Room almost filled. I settled into a chair next to the entrance so I would have a full view of the audience and, as I liked to do in the semidarkness, I would be able to look for the figure of Abraham or follow the exploits of Cyrus the Great on the tapestries during the concert.

When the small orchestra was settled around the piano, I was stunned to see another cellist in Carla's place. Tony was the last musician to arrive and, heading toward the Steinway at a fast pace, he gave his usual simple nod toward the audience.

Applause, then the concert began. Works by Hayden, Beethoven, and Schubert were to be performed. A small card inside the program gave a biography of the cellist who was replacing Carla. I thought Carla must be ill or detained by a more important engagement. I noticed, however, that the young musician replacing her was not a novice. He was already first cellist with the Tchaikovsky Chamber Orchestra and had just participated in the Marlboro Summer Music Festival in Vermont.

As always, I was enchanted with the concert. I never knew if it was because of the music, the musicians or the venue—it didn't matter. I was beginning to understand why so many people came to the Isabella Stewart Gardner Museum, a reconstructed Venetian palace. One simply felt comfortable there, far from the tumultuous world, sheltered from the outside and the winter weather while listening to good music, which of course is synonymous with classical music.

As we had planned, after the concert I was to find Tony and Carla downstairs on the main floor near the large staircase. Tony had told me on the phone, "We will meet you there, but take advantage of the time to tour the museum while Carla and I change and settle some questions we have with Joel Cohen about the Wednesday night concert at the Church of the Covenant."

Once the concert was finished, I went down the grand staircase among the people headed toward the cloakroom. I hesitated, trying to decide between going all the way to the Spanish cloister, up to *El Jaleo*, the large painting by John Singer Sargent, where I always discovered something new in the face and the movement of the Andalusian dancers, or to rest a few moments wandering in the interior courtyard and garden. After standing in line and getting my overcoat from the cloakroom, I decided to go sit on the large windowsill facing the patio. At this time of year, and according to the testamentary dispositions of Mrs. Gardner herself, the interior garden is entirely decorated with white flowers; enormous pots of poinsettias and hydrangeas are placed at the foot of the columns and around the fountains. And because of the glass ceiling on top of the fifth floor that encloses the garden like a greenhouse, there is a white, leaded light that shines through to the lobby. The atmosphere is almost moist. To me, it seemed quite different from that of the palaces in Venice I had visited for the first time many winters ago; I had never found the same transparency or the airiness of the light, nor the brisk air that came from the Adriatic that blows through the galleries in Venice. But here, at the Isabella Stewart Gardner Museum, the surreal atmosphere that emanated from the patio went well with all the fabulous accumulated treasures, as if they were in a large safe and every visitor had a key to unlock the museum's precious objects and masterpieces.

I stopped daydreaming. As planned, I went toward the grand staircase. Tony was already at the bottom of the stairs but without Carla. As always, Tony was smiling.

He was still wearing his tuxedo under the old, long raincoat he always wore open, even in winter. Traces of perspiration could be seen on his shirt, and a strand of hair was stuck on his still sweaty forehead. He hadn't showered or changed. In spite of his smile, he appeared tired.

Tony said, "I was waiting and looking for you. Things finally went faster than planned."

I didn't ask any questions about Carla, and Tony suggested we walk to the apartment. The rain had stopped, and, as often happens in Boston at this time of year, the air suddenly became warm and humid. We were alone on the sidewalk in the section of the Fenway bordering the elegant buildings built at the beginning of the century. Today they were neglected by their owners and invaded by hordes of students. Tony and Carla's place was at the end of the street near the intersection of Boylston Street.

Once we arrived at his building, while looking for his keys in his raincoat pockets, Tony abruptly said, "We will eat alone tonight. I didn't want to cancel our dinner. Carla has left for Philadelphia. She found a job with the Philadelphia Orchestra and was hired at her first audition."

We had to climb stairs to a monumental stone porch to reach the entrance to the building, which opened into a vast vestibule. It was decorated with mirrors and old wall lamps here and there that cast a weak light on a few old velvet armchairs, vestiges of a past era. A grill-caged elevator with a seat inside, the kind manufactured by Otis at the turn of the century, took us slowly to the third floor where Tony and Carla rented an apartment. It had three spacious rooms that overlooked the Fenway's small trees in the Back Bay. They had been linked together and must have been part of a larger residence during the Edwardian Era.

The apartment exuded an atmosphere of space and distinction, perhaps because of the high ceilings, perhaps because of the tall white marble fireplace, or perhaps because of the deep bow window without curtains that allowed a view of the avenue and the woods.

A small table with only two chairs had been set in front of the bay window. Tony asked if I would light the fire while he changed his clothes and took care of reheating the dinner.

Now dressed in a striped shirt, a V-neck sweater, and freshly washed jeans, Tony came back from the kitchen holding two glasses and a bottle of California Chardonnay. He had remembered that I liked this white wine and that I liked to drink it ice cold. Judging from the condensation on the glasses, he had apparently put them in the freezer.

The walk, the fire in the fireplace, the clean clothes, and the Chardonnay made Tony look much better, and he seemed happy to be home. Could it also be the prospect of our meeting? I sensed that Tony felt a need to talk.

Handing me my glass, Tony said, "You know, I should be sad tonight. Carla and I have never been separated, and tonight, for the first time in ten years, I am alone. Carla had the courage to leave. I was hurt at the time but, deep down, I knew we would end up this way. Now I'm aware that her decision will have a positive effect on my life. I sense that her departure is pushing me to act, to come out of this mediocrity that I was sinking into and dragging her with me. Carla is much more talented than I am. She is stronger than I am. She should succeed in her career, and I was holding her back."

"What about your own career, Tony? With all the concerts and all the lessons you give, it's a wonder you have time to compose anything."

Tony didn't answer right away. He went to the couch facing the armchair where I was sitting, put his glass on the floor, and said seriously, "I insisted on having this dinner tonight, even without Carla, because I'm leaving also. I've decided to get out of Boston."

Tony must have realized that the announcement about his departure was too brusque, that it might upset me, because he added quickly: "With your line of work and with mine, I am sure we will have the opportunity to find each other. Somewhere in the world, while I am on tour and you are at another bank in another city, we will meet once again."

Tony was quiet for a moment and then said slowly: "I wanted to thank you."

"I don't believe I did much for you, Tony," I replied. "It's you who did a lot for me. I knew very few people when I arrived in Boston, and you and Carla welcomed me with your friendship. I am sad to hear the news of your separation. When I saw you together, I never suspected anything. It's something I could not have imagined. I thought you were both very attached to each other and to this city."

"You know, it's very difficult to succeed here," Tony interjected. "The Boston public is very conservative. They don't like contemporary music very much. I have a lot of trouble getting my compositions published. It'll be easier in New York. Maybe, after all, Carla did think about me and my career first."

While Tony was expressing his hope to start his life over in another city, I thought to myself that Carla had decided to start her life over by leaving for Philadelphia. Although from a family of Bostonians for several generations, Tony shared the belief that one can change one's life, start over from zero, and succeed. This is the dream Americans chase by moving to a new city, to a new state, crossing new frontiers. For them, going somewhere else means a rebirth and taking on a new identity.

Tony continued in a convincing tone, "I'll be thirty-five years old soon. I think I can leave and make something of myself. I'm going to move to

New York where I have a few friends. To begin with, while I audition to find work playing in an orchestra, I'll live with an old friend who had studied at the Berklee School of Music in Boston. But I don't want to play every night. I want to have time to compose and sell what I've already written. I think it'll be easier to find a publisher in New York because my music doesn't seem to interest anyone here."

"Yet I've never seen so many music schools as I've seen here in Boston," I commented.

"That's true. I wonder if it's because Boston is content with training musicians. The city is known for the best music schools in the world, but it doesn't do much for young composers. You've seen the programs. It's always Beethoven!"

"Most often directed to perfection. You know, I would have very much liked to have heard Charles Munch. I would've liked to find myself at the Symphony on a snowy night when Charles Munch was conducting the Ninth. Diane Kitchell, whom I met at the Friends of Symphony and who knew Charles Munch well, told me that the whole orchestra was captivated and uplifted by him. You could feel it in the auditorium, and the audience reacted in the same way the orchestra did. Even so, there is some of Boulez's music at Symphony Hall from time to time, but only when he is actually here. When he gave two concerts there at the beginning of the winter, I went to both of them. But it's true, I saw mostly students there."

"You already know that Bostonians don't much like innovation. It's the same with art. Very few galleries will take the risk of displaying a young painter's works. They prefer to support the artists' paintings that will sell well. The public always wants the same subjects: the New England countryside, seascapes, the coast of Maine, houses on Cape Cod and portraits— many portraits."

"It's simply because Bostonians like the authenticity of their life and feel deeply that there's no need to transform it," I countered. "Besides, I have observed that this realism is required, even of artists who are not from here. I think of Rockwell Kent. And also, the works of Edward Hopper.

57

The boulders of Maine and the dunes of South Truro can hardly be magnified. Why change nature that surrounds you? It's beautiful and strong as it is."

"You're perhaps right. Maybe that's why Boston artists excel in portraits. There's nothing to modify, only to enhance certain traits."

"Actually, there are some admirable portraits in Boston. I saw some superb ones at the 'Exhibit of Bostonians at the End of the 1930s' organized by the Museum of Fine Arts. It included works not only by Sargent but by other artists whose names I've forgotten. I remember a painting of a young woman wearing a fur hat adorned with an enormous red rose. It was worthy of Gainsborough. I also remember the portrait of a young cellist wearing a maroon suit that made me think of the *Jeune Homme* of Bronzino. I think the tradition of portraits still continues today: I have seen some lovely paintings by current artists."

"It's a bit different today," Tony replied. "Before it was Beacon Hill society, the people from Back Bay, the old families from Boston; now it's the Harvard professors who seek to have their portraits painted. It's less worldly, less refined, but it's always as academic."

"I think you resent your city a little," I remarked.

"Most likely because I didn't succeed here. Boston is a difficult city; it doesn't support anything except excellence."

Tony picked up his glass, got up from the sofa, and said, "I'm a little ashamed to admit it, but since Carla has left, I've started to compose again, and I'd like to write an opera. I know I'll have some work in New York! Now, it's time to get something to eat. I prepared something I know how to make, grilled sea bass. I bought the fish and some oysters at Legal Seafood."

We hardly tasted the oysters, and the grilled sea bass Tony had taken such care to prepare was left almost untouched. However, we did finish the bottle of Chardonnay.

After dinner Tony went toward the small room adjacent to the parlor that served as an office and reception area. A piano occupied the whole space, and a large bookcase covered one wall. He returned with a book.

"I wanted to give you this book. It's a book about Gershwin, our only great musician. I know that you like him a lot, certainly more than I do."

"I admire him very much because he embodies America!"

"You're perhaps right to admire him. *Rhapsody in Blue* is one of the greatest works of the twentieth century. Maybe you already know that Gershwin met Ravel, whom he revered greatly, and the French musician had some influence on him. Both their concertos for piano have many melodies in common. Both of their works are overwhelming. Gershwin is extremely well liked by the French, and he owes them something. I would like you to keep this book as a souvenir of our friendship."

And as if I too were captivated by Tony's enthusiasm for starting his new life in New York and seeing his hopes come true, without thinking I told him, "As for me, I will make a wish: that one day your music will be played first at Carnegie Hall and then here, at Symphony Hall, just like Gershwin's, because I'm sure you will come back."

"I don't know. But you, you will come back because you'll succeed here."

Tony was quiet. He seemed to be concentrating: did he see himself at Symphony Hall, bowing to the crowd that was applauding him? Then, as he had the habit of doing for important things, all of a sudden he said, "I wanted to thank you with this dinner tonight. I wanted to tell you that every time I noticed you while I was playing at the Four Seasons Hotel on Sunday afternoons, it was a great comfort to me. It was also…."

I interrupted him. I was not surprised by what Tony was saying, but I didn't want to hear more. I had a habit of going to the Four Seasons anonymously. I was well aware that Tony would see me from behind his piano, but I wanted to keep that a secret. Neither he nor I were going to stay in Boston for a very long time. Tony had just announced his departure for New York, and he would be leaving soon. And my internship at the bank was only for one year. Confessions at this point were useless.

In a detached manner, I hurried to add: "As far as I'm concerned, I always thought, 'Tony deserves better than this.' I had promised myself to talk to you about it, to give you advice and encouragement."

Tony took his time to respond. He had become calm, and in his eyes I noticed the authority he had when he would come onto the stage, going toward his piano in a rapid and brisk pace. "I would notice you when I would turn to face the audience. No doubt you believed that I didn't see you way at the back of the huge parlor. It was the one scattered with large armchairs and facing the Public Garden. When I was at the Four Seasons, I was playing for you. I terminated my contract with the hotel yesterday."

It must've been a little later than ten o'clock when I left Tony's house on the Fenway. Tony wanted to accompany me, but I discouraged him, preferring to say goodbye inside rather than on the street; I thought it was better that way. We shook hands and stood facing each other for a moment without saying anything, as if all had been said.

When I passed through the door of the building, when I started walking on the shiny sidewalk, when I breathed in the humid and almost warm smell of the Back Bay Fenway woods, I felt better, almost relieved of a burden that was weighing me down. I had said everything I could say. I had done everything I could do. Tony's life and mine were going in different directions, as if we could do nothing about it.

I needed to regain the quiet and sweetness of the night. The heavy rains that had fallen until evening had washed and calmed everything: the trees, the billboards, the building facades, the cars. My body and spirit were obsessed by the prospect of walking home in the Back Bay. I let this sensation overtake me. I needed to walk and let all that was around me permeate my being. I knew that this old habit of walking would give me the resources I needed to help get rid of the hole I felt in the pit of my stomach. In the same way others would regain some calm by driving for hours, for me it was the city that would dominate and soothe my senses.

After crossing Massachusetts Avenue, I knew I would take Boylston Street. I would go by the Conservatory of Music before getting to the Institute of Contemporary Art. There, in front of the museum I would make a first stop. I would pause for a while to look at the posters announcing the upcoming exhibits. Then, after passing by the fire station that, no matter what the weather, always had its doors wide open showing the two enormous red trucks ready to speed out, I would turn left. I would arrive on Newbury Street and continue to Clarendon Street, always making a second stop in front of Childs Gallery.

Most of the art galleries on Newbury Street have their windows lighted at night. The Childs Gallery was different from all the others, displaying only one brightly lit painting. A few days earlier I had been captivated by the painting in their window: it was a picture of Boston covered with snow, a view of the Public Garden, barely outlined against a white, fluffy, bright background. Under the frame, there was a small card with the artist's name that I hadn't noticed the last time: Mary Coolidge Adams.

Arriving at the end of Newbury Street, I crossed diagonally left to reach Clarendon Street, dominated by the towers of the First Baptist Church, which let me know that I had almost arrived home. From the Commonwealth Avenue Square I could see the Public Garden gates, and on the opposite side, through the magnolias stripped of foliage and a few feet from the garden, I noticed the Victorian façade of the sandstone house and windows where I lived on the third floor.

Before finishing my walk, I would stop one last time, not because my legs were aching, not because I was tired, but for the pleasure I felt each time I reached this point at the intersection of Commonwealth and Clarendon. I would stop there as if I wanted to take in and contemplate Commonwealth Avenue like a huge river: grand, deep, steady, and majestic.

Only a few houses are still occupied on this part of the avenue. Similar to Charles Street, it's on winter nights that Commonwealth Avenue rediscovers the beauty of its origins, when it has been abandoned by pedestrians and automobiles, when it's lighted only by the old gas street lamps, witnesses to its birth, when the fine powdery snow covers the distinctive building facades, erasing the wrinkles of time and the warts of the century.

I soon reached my house, climbed the porch steps, and passed through the front door. In the entry, the lantern on the small table next to the elevator shed a golden light that made the mahogany doors and the furniture in the lobby glow with a red shadow. I didn't take the elevator. I preferred to walk up the grand staircase, pass the Corinthian columns on the second-floor landing, and then from this level, lean over the ramp and glance down at the circular swoop of the elegant bannister and staircase. Then I'd continue up to my apartment door on the third floor.

I liked my apartment to be dimly lit when I returned home. When I would leave in the evening, I'd always leave one or two lamps on in the living room and in my bedroom. And when I came home, I liked to sit on the sofa in the living room for a moment to smoke a cigarette and look at the spacious, dark sky above Boston through the window where the shades were raised. The only part of the city I could see were the rooftops covered with snow, but at night I could see and imagine all kinds of visible and invisible images, like the blinking lights that sprinkled my dreams, like those of the airplanes circling Logan Airport.

Once in a while I'd open the window a little to inhale the scent of the ocean. From the Back Bay, the neighborhood built on old marshlands, you can't see the water. It's as if the neighborhood is turning its back to the sea. But on certain evenings the ocean smell penetrates the gaping space of Boston Common, reaching all the way to me so that I could taste salt on my lips.

I'd listen to one or two tapes, mostly jazz but sometimes also music from movies. It was almost always the same ones, except when Joe, my Italian colleague from the Bank of Boston, would bring me his latest recordings that reflected his tastes more than mine, tapes that he would leave in my mailbox early in the morning.

It's thanks to him that I discovered Anita Baker, Dionne Warwick, Regina Belle, and others. Joe would spend his evenings recording, either from the radio or from his own cassettes. He meticulously marked the date and time of each recording on the label stuck to the small plastic box containing the tape: January 14 – 10 p.m., January 20 – 11:30 p.m., January 23 – 2:30 a.m., January 24 – 3 a.m., January 29 – 4:40 a.m. When I would see the number of *ante meridiem* designations or the recordings before noon increase, I thought that Joe's anxieties must also be increasing, but Joe, who was mildly depressed by Boston winters, had a tendency to exaggerate.

I took the tape that Joe had brought me that morning. It was Anita Baker and on the label was written January 30 – 1 a.m. The title of the first song seemed a coincidence to me: "Giving You the Best That I Got."

I went to get the book on Gershwin I had left on the hall table, the book Tony had given me, and then I sat on the sofa to listen to Anita Baker.

I started thinking about this last evening with Tony. He was leaving for New York, my training at the bank would be ending soon and I would be leaving Boston. Would we ever see each other again? I would've liked to have told him more about my thoughts, but I hadn't, thinking it was too late to do so.

There are encounters in life that are brief but that have an everlasting effect. I've learned that because we know these encounters will soon end, we tend to give them the best of ourselves.

I started leafing through the book on Gershwin and came across a black-and-white photo of Tony that had been slipped between the pages. He was young, quite handsome at the beginning of his career, wearing his concert tuxedo, a white wing-collared shirt, a smiling face, soft and generous eyes, and a determined chin.

The photo was signed by Bachrach, and there was also a short listing of Tony's first successes: the titles, the prizes, the first concerts, the first recordings, the first compositions.

After knowing Tony and after our time together tonight, how could I ever forget the Isabella Stewart Gardner Museum?

7

UNCLE CHARLES AND
THE SINGING BEACH

I met Mary at the French Library during a lecture by Stanley Hoffmann on the French Revolution. I still remember the title, "The French Revolution Is Over." The last time I saw her, the look in Mary's eyes told me that something was upsetting her. She seemed less attentive, thinner and somewhat tired.

The mutual friend who had introduced us told me that her father had taken a bad fall at the beginning of January and he was having trouble recovering. His name was Charles Elianos, but everyone called him Uncle Charles (this confirmed my observation that Anglo-Saxons often use a familiar form of address).

Since the death of his second wife about ten years before, Uncle Charles had come to live with his only daughter, Mary, from his first marriage. Mary, who had never married, was a professor of French at Pine Manor, a small private college for women in the Boston area.

Mary had taken one of the two rooms in the Brookline apartment she rented and made it available to her father. She had given up her own bedroom and installed herself in the living room. She slept on the sofa and they shared the bathroom. She said her father's presence didn't bother her. On the contrary, it was company that she appreciated at the end of the afternoon after coming from her classes at Pine Manor.

For ten years and right up to early this winter, nothing had disturbed their new life and the routine they had established between them. Their shared life had brought them closer. I believe they both thought this situation would last much longer.

At the beginning of each December, Uncle Charles would leave for Florida to visit his sister Helen, who had settled there when her husband retired. He would be there for Christmas and then would stay one month, sometimes two, happy to be with the younger sister he had arranged to bring to the United States only a few years after his own arrival. During the summer, to escape the heavy heat of Boston, he would go to Maine or Nova Scotia, where he liked the brisk air and sparsely populated islands.

Mary continued to enjoy her freedom. She took advantage of the rich winter seasons in Boston by going out often, never missing concerts at Symphony Hall, exhibits at the Museum of Fine Arts, or the many lectures around the city. She also made the most of Boston summers because, unlike her father, she enjoyed the area's typical humid heat. With the first nice days of spring, when her classes at the college ended, she would not go home to Brookline right away, but drove her old Toyota around the Boston beaches. Sometimes she would go as far as Cape Cod and wouldn't return home until the evening when she felt cooled, refreshed, and relaxed.

During all this time Uncle Charles remained active, alert, and in good health despite his advanced age. He seemed happy. As for Mary, she discovered that her father was a pleasant companion who was easy to be around. In addition, she found him to be loving and considerate, something she had never known about her father before. Even with Uncle Charles's presence, her routine continued throughout the course of the years, and she would sometimes ask herself if these years with her old father were the best she had ever known.

Several days after returning from a trip to Canada—it must have been a couple of months ago in September—Uncle Charles started complaining about a pain in his abdomen. His stomach had swollen, one leg hurt, and he had difficulty walking. Mary drove him to the Massachusetts General Hospital, and after a series of tests, the doctor's diagnosis was definite: he had a cancerous tumor, and chances of survival following an operation would be two to three years. Mary asked them to operate but not to tell her father how serious his condition was. She decided they would continue as if everything were the same.

Uncle Charles stayed at the hospital for about ten days. When he returned to the little apartment in Brookline, he realized that their life's routine had changed: he was condemned to spend the winter in Boston, and Mary had to give up the activities she loved.

Without saying anything, each one tried to cope with the new situation. Mary called the Visiting Nurse Association, who sent a nurse every morning and evening to give Uncle Charles his meds. Each week she would fill the freezer with meals, and during the weekend she would take her father out to a restaurant. As for Uncle Charles, he seemed to be doing better since his operation in September, and once a week he went to Mass General by himself. He would call a taxi that would drive him to the entrance of the building and then, once his treatment was finished, the taxi would bring him back home. He continued to prepare his lunch methodically, to read the *Boston Globe* from the first page to the last, to watch the elegant Christopher Lydon on television (whose biting analysis he appreciated), and to bet on Governor Dukakis's chance of getting into the White House.

Everyone wondered how long this new stage could last. The doctor's prognosis was for about two to three years, and Uncle Charles was not suffering yet.

But with the onset of the first cold spell and the first snowstorm, things changed. During the first week of January, almost four months after the operation, while leaving Mass General to meet his taxi, Uncle Charles slipped on a patch of ice. He was brought to the emergency room and then to the operating arena. Uncle Charles had broken his leg. This time he remained in the hospital for two long months. The endless hours of rehabilitation he was forced to undergo barely improved his condition: he could hardly walk any more. His morale declined. Mary decided to bring him back home. It was now March and, as often happens in Boston, the winter weather got worse.

I had expected to see Mary at the small reception following the French Library lecture, but she must have left right at the end of Stanley Hoffmann's talk. Uncle Charles's condition had perhaps gotten worse. I telephoned Mary as soon as I got home.

"Uncle Charles isn't very well," she told me. "He has trouble walking, so he won't be able to go out in this kind of weather. He just takes a few steps here and there around the apartment."

"Does he get bored? The day must seem very long for him."

"He reads less, much less," she replied.

"But I'm sure he must follow the presidential campaign on television. Dukakis has separated himself from the pack. The latest primaries are good for him, so Uncle Charles must be happy."

"He continues to watch it, but he sometimes falls asleep."

"You know, Mary, I was calling to suggest that I come take care of …." but I immediately corrected myself by saying, "I wanted to tell you that I can come to keep your father company next Saturday. I'm free all day. I could arrive around ten o'clock and have lunch with him. That way, if you have errands to do in Boston, you can do them."

"Uncle Charles will be very happy to see you," she replied. It was as if she'd been waiting for this offer that would allow her to have a little rest after the past few months, and before facing those that were yet to come that would be even harder.

"Don't come too early. The nurse arrives at ten o'clock. Come after that. Uncle Charles can open the apartment door for you."

It had snowed a lot in Boston during this first week of March. When I arrived at the small street that led to Mary's building in Brookline, the parking lot in front of their apartment had been cleared of snow and I had no difficulty finding the space that was reserved for them, but the sidewalk had not been shoveled, and I had trouble walking. They lived in one of the rare small buildings in this residential neighborhood that is scattered with huge houses set in the middle of large parks, so common in Boston. A sign at the space reserved for them had their names on it. Mary had already left so the parking space was empty.

I went toward the "B" door of the building. It was open; the security code wasn't needed until nighttime. I entered the small vestibule that was more like a narrow corridor with an elevator and staircase at the end.

I was about to ring for the elevator when I saw Uncle Charles sitting on the steps of the staircase. He was dressed in his overcoat, a scarf knotted around his raised collar, and a hat on his head. He was smiling at me. "But what are you doing here, Uncle Charles? I thought you couldn't leave the apartment!"

"You know, I can walk," he said in a derisive tone. But, smiling again, he added, "I could only get this far. Unfortunately, now I can't move. In fact I was waiting for you because you're going to have to help me get up."

I had trouble getting Uncle Charles to stand; although he had lost a lot of weight, he was still heavy. When I placed my hands under his arms to lift him, I sensed that his force and his will were far from extinguished. Once standing in his checkered navy blue overcoat, wearing his black felt hat, holding himself very straight—at least as straight as he could—Uncle Charles didn't look at all like an old man, much more like an old actor who had not yet left the stage.

One small step at a time we reached the elevator.

"You see, I can walk," Uncle Charles said again. "But this is enough for today. Let's go back to the apartment."

Once we arrived, he let go of my arm and started walking alone, straight to the armchair that was in front of the television. The room wasn't large. It had a low ceiling and everything was orderly. The sofa where Mary slept was covered with a throw and maroon velvet cushions. On the table where they ate their meals were two place settings separated by a small red poinsettia.

"Stay seated, Uncle Charles," I said. "I'm going to help you take off your coat. Don't move. Instead, tell me what you were going to do outside in such terrible weather."

He hesitated to answer. It was as if he had a guilty conscience. He had betrayed his daughter who had forbidden him to go out. He was afraid to appear senile because he had made an error in judgment by overestimating his strength. But once the nurse had left, didn't he have the strength to shave, get dressed, get some money and his keys, go all the way to the elevator, and take it to reach the first floor? Once there, his strength left him, and all of a sudden the project of going out into the street on such a cold day didn't seem sensible.

"I wanted to go a few blocks to the grocery store to buy a bottle of wine. I know the French can't do without it when they have lunch or dinner. I would've had some with you. I haven't had a glass of wine for months because of the medication and because Mary is very strict about this."

"Do you want me to turn the television on while I put the meals in the microwave? Or do you prefer to read the newspaper?"

"I've already read it," responded Uncle Charles, who seemed surprised by the question; he had read his newspaper before seven in the morning all his life.

But had he really read it? I noticed that the *Globe* was on the low table in front of the couch, still in its plastic bag and still wet here and there from melting snowflakes.

I suspected he had certainly read the doubt in my eyes. He acted as if it was business as usual, and to show that he was up to date on current events said quickly: "Do you believe Michael Dukakis will be elected?"

Knowing that Uncle Charles remained faithful to his Greek origins, that he had known the governor's father, Dr. Panos Dukakis, who had an office in the neighborhood where they lived, and that Mary kept up with Michael's elderly mother, Euterpe Dukakis, who would come to Pine Manor from time to time, I replied: "He has a good chance of carrying it. I believe

Americans want a little more social justice. He's capable of making reforms, and he's a just and reasonable man."

"Well, as for myself," said Uncle Charles, "I think that 'Duke' will never be king. I wish he would win, but he will never be elected. His ideas are good, he has done an extraordinary job of improving Massachusetts, and he is sincere and totally honest. But he's too Greek; he's small and dark like a Greek person. The Americans will elect a president who looks like them. And the Democrats will finish by finding a blond and blue-eyed candidate."

Uncle Charles was reading less, he hardly ever telephoned, and he often fell asleep in front of the television as if the news of the world no longer concerned him, but in spite of this, when he wanted to express his point of view, he seemed to have conserved all his memory, all his judgment, all his vocabulary, and all his clarity. I became aware of his keen mind and his vigorous spirit when we were at the table and he started telling me about his life: his childhood in Salonika, his arrival in New York in 1920, his first jobs, how he became an accountant at Filene's department store in Boston, how he created his own company, how he bought his first car, his first house. He seemed happy to remember these different stages of a life that spanned nearly a century of major upheavals and wars. As it was for many Americans, unlike for most Europeans, these events hadn't seemed to reverse the normal everyday course of things and had only scratched the surface of his life. He had done many things, and he had loved life.

But the recounting of his life ended, and all of a sudden his face became somber.

"I'm going to leave soon," he said briskly. "For me it's only a question of weeks, maybe days. The time has come to leave this place."

"No, no," I responded. "You're doing much better, you're beginning to walk and, as soon as it's nice, you'll be able to go out again."

"There are many things I'd like to see again before leaving, but there is one I would like above all else, and I feel I have the strength to do it. One last time I'd like to walk on the beach, on the small beach in

Manchester-by-the-Sea, the one they call the Singing Beach. You know it, of course. The ocean's magnificent there, both tumultuous and then suddenly tranquil, a reflection of life, mysterious and at the same time open, and in the summer we hear the voices and laughter of children in the waves and in the surf. It's the beach that sings. Can you drive me there?"

"That seems possible. We'd have to wrap you up and take some good shoes. The trip isn't long, but we'd have to do it when the weather isn't as bad as it is today."

"In 1939 when we arrived in Boston I'd go there often with Maria and Mary, who had just turned ten years old. We'd go almost every Sunday. We'd take the train at North Station and get off at Manchester-by-the-Sea's small station. Later when I bought everyone bicycles, we'd put them on the train, get off two or three stops before Manchester, continue by bicycle, and once there we'd picnic on the beach. My wife, Maria, adored these excursions. She was a superb woman and very athletic."

"It's true that Route 127 is magnificent when it winds along the ocean after Beverly," I said. "I sometimes drive there on Sundays too. I am attracted by this side of Boston also. The North Shore seems more Bostonian to me than the South Shore, more impressive and more austere."

"When we leave we have to say goodbye to the places we loved," continued Uncle Charles, still very serious. "To say adieu, to see them one last time is as difficult as leaving those you've loved and those who loved you. What good does it do to get better for a few more days just to sink down even deeper? When it's time, you have to take your bow and leave the stage."

"Uncle Charles, don't be pessimistic! Do you remember when I came to see you at Mass General after your first operation in September? You said to me, 'Once I can walk, we'll go back to Lock-Ober, my favorite restaurant, for a grand lunch. We'll have a gala meal.'"

I hesitated to express my thoughts that seemed a little out of place to me, but I felt I had to do it: "You know, Uncle Charles, I believe there is something else after, another existence, another world that awaits us."

"We've never talked about these things before," he said. "But you see me coming to the end, and for me life is the only thing I am sure of. I am not religious; I lost my faith when I was a kid, when I left for America. The day I took the boat at Salonika, I understood I had to abandon all the old beliefs to start a new life in a new world. And once I arrived in America, I had to work hard and fight to live. It was difficult to think of anything else."

"You wanted to succeed and you did!"

Uncle Charles smiled again and added: "We Greeks, we left without our popes! The Irish came with their priests. Even your Franco friends from Quebec brought their priests with them and also the good sisters who taught school to their children. That is how they kept their faith and their language. Me, I no longer have a church, or rituals, or the desire to go back there. But I'm sure that once I'm gone, there will always be life, there will always be the ocean and God, who will be there on the other side, and who will not be involved with the business of men and their petty affairs. He has much better things to do."

After lunch Uncle Charles needed to lie down for a few minutes. He said he wasn't tired, that he hated to sleep after eating, that a nap was only good for lazy people, but that the prone position would be good for his back. He had to stretch his legs, especially his left leg that still hurt him near the hip.

While Uncle Charles was resting in the small bedroom, I cleared the table. Once the dishes were loaded into the dishwasher, I sat down to rest a little myself. I took the *Globe* out of its plastic bag; the headline about Dukakis's victory in the New Hampshire primary was in big letters.

Shortly after, I got up to look into his room and opened the door Uncle Charles had left ajar. I saw him, fully dressed, sleeping peacefully on his big bed; he had loosened his tie, his mouth was open, arms stretched down along the side of his body, his breathing causing his chest to rise and fall in an even rhythm. I approached the bed. I wanted to admire his handsome face, sculpted by so many years of work and effort. His features were relaxed, his whole face seemed peaceful. I didn't see any signs of aging or sickness there. Had he been expecting an end when he closed his eyes?

It was almost three o'clock. I could leave now, before nightfall. Mary would be home shortly and the anonymous nurse would soon be there.

I still had a little time left. I could have stayed a few minutes longer, but I preferred to leave while Uncle Charles was sleeping. I didn't feel like meeting Mary and the nurse because I knew I would have to speak to them, to tell them that Uncle Charles was doing better, that I would come back to get him and keep him company as soon as it was nice, and we would take a ride all the way to Manchester. I didn't feel like pretending to believe his health would improve and we could make plans. But it wasn't that either, because there was an implied agreement between Uncle Charles and me. Would I have had the courage or the guts to tell them that Uncle Charles had already accepted his demise and some plans had already been made? Uncle Charles knew what to expect with death; we were both clear on that. But it was different with God; nothing seemed settled yet. We had to continue that discussion.

I asked myself if I would have the time to drive him to Manchester and to take him all the way to the Singing Beach.

Although it was already March, we couldn't count on the weather improving. Uncle Charles undoubtedly wouldn't be able to walk on the beach but he could stay warm sitting in the car. I would drive him as close as possible to the ocean. I knew the small road that goes up to the Singing Beach well, and I knew that it ended at a bluff where it is forbidden to park during the summer months. From there the view is dominated by the immense ocean, green, raw, streaked with large white blade-like waves; on the left are two small rocky islands, and in the distance a view of the Cape Ann shores and the Beauport lighthouse. Would this be enough for Uncle Charles?

When I left the building, I saw that, with night approaching, snow had started to fall. My car was already covered with a fine white powder. I searched the glove compartment for a small plastic ice scraper to remove the snow accumulating on the windshield and the rear window.

I started the motor and I was just about to leave when, looking through the rearview mirror to back up, I heard a knock at the door and saw, almost stuck against the window, the face of a young man. I opened the window part way, and the young man asked me if I was going to Boston and, if so, could I drop him off at Boston College.

I wasn't in the habit of picking up hitchhikers, but the appearance of this young man seemed serious; most likely he was one of the many students responsible for the increase in Boston's population during the winter, so I agreed.

I felt as though I had a need to get in touch with life, to speak with people in good health, who are only preoccupied with their immediate future, their work, their family, their trivial concerns, as if everyday life should not change, should not stop.

After placing his big bag under the seat, my passenger sat next to me. Looking at him more closely, I became aware that he was not a student but a man past his thirties. His face was smooth and dark, with finely shaped eyebrows and a very straight nose. The chin was a bit plump but the eyes had a decisive air about them. His brown hair, pushed back, revealed a wide forehead that exposed the look of a strong-willed character.

He introduced himself; the cadence of his voice was fast and clipped:

"Kevin O'Brian, I work at Boston College. My mother lives in this development but in building C, which is right behind the one you came out of. I thank you very much for your kindness because I hardly felt like taking the T in this weather. Thank you for dropping me off at the Reservoir. Boston College is right next to it."

"I am going to Back Bay," I replied. "It's nothing for me to take a detour by the Reservoir; I'll drop you off at your door."

"Do you come here to Brookline often?" he asked.

"Fairly rarely, but today I stayed a lot longer. I was with a sick friend keeping him company."

"I hope it's not serious."

It was hard for me to respond. Is old age a sickness? I didn't feel like digressing about age, senior citizens, old people, people who are dependent, so I restricted myself to saying: "No, it's just a question of time."

"I come every Saturday to have lunch with my mother. She's been living here for a dozen years. Before my parents divorced, we lived in Dorchester. Do you know Dorchester?"

Actually, I didn't know this suburb on the ocean south of Boston very well. I had gone to the Kennedy Library, which was built directly on the harbor, a few times. As I drove my car through Dorchester, I had never lingered in what appeared to be a poor and dreary Irish suburb.

As we were driving east along Route 9, the high walls of the Reservoir appeared, and the many traffic lights signaled that we were already in Boston. We had to stop repeatedly. I turned toward my neighbor and noticed that he had removed his scarf and unbuttoned his overcoat. He was wearing a white sweater with a rolled collar and his flannel suit was a dark grey, almost black.

"After my classes I go to Dorchester every chance I get," he said. "There's a bathhouse on the beach there that's open all year round. After a nice sauna, it's great to jump into the cold water. I miss it when I can't go."

Laughing, he continued: "The ocean is like a magnet that attracts me, and my joy increases as I get closer to Dorchester, where I can see the waves between the two large Boston Gas tanks. I'm sure the many people who commute to this place imagine, as I do, that the gigantic rainbow painted by Corita Kent on the walls of the gas tank means that eventually there is sunshine in life, and you have to be there to seize the opportunity."

"It's a privilege for Boston to be situated near the ocean," I said mechanically.

"The ocean is part of my moral and physical health! It gives me balance and it also teaches me to broaden my horizons."

After a moment of silence, as if to stress the most important part of his words, he added slowly: "The ocean helps us to go toward God."

Then, wanting to bring his remarks back to more simple proportions, he earnestly added: "Please be assured, I belong to Boston College and not to one of those sects that seizes every opportunity to preach and that are so prevalent in America! I see that we're arriving. You can leave me there in front of the building next to the large gated entrance. Here's my card."

On the small business card I read:

Kevin O'Brian, SJ
Professor of Theology, Boston College
Chestnut Hill, MA 02167

Father Kevin reached the gate in a few strides, but just before going through, he turned and waved to me. I answered by waving back to let him know I had received his message. I now knew what I had to do. From that moment on, everything was clear to me. There was no confusion about the messenger, or about the content of his message. I had just met my messenger, and Uncle Charles knew his.

There was not another minute to lose. I had made up my mind.

As soon as I arrive home in Back Bay tonight, I'll call Mary and tell her that I will come to get Uncle Charles and, as he has asked, I will drive him to Manchester-by-the-Sea. We will tour along the Singing Beach and look at the ocean. Tomorrow is Sunday. I'll get him tomorrow morning. He'll have to be wrapped in warm clothing and wear sturdy shoes.

8

LUNCH AT THE SOMERSET

Last week I received a telephone call from my friend Eliza Stein, who lives in a small town in New Hampshire. She let me know that she was coming to Boston as she does two or three times every winter. Generally she only stays a few days to see the doctor, buy books, spend some time at the big city libraries, and go to the symphony. She doesn't book a hotel or stay with friends but likes to stay at the Chilton instead. It's a women's club named after Mary Chilton, the first woman on the Mayflower to arrive in Boston.

Eliza said to me: "I can't invite you to lunch at the Chilton as I usually do. The dining room is closed because of work being done, but due to an agreement between the two clubs, I can invite you to the Somerset." She then added in a half-serious, half-joking tone, "The Somerset always balks at admitting women, but they will be forced to accept the recent Supreme Court decision, which is irrevocable. Come on Tuesday—I'll wait for you at noon."

I was happy to accept her invitation, eager to have a pleasant moment with Eliza. I liked to listen to her recount stories of her life in Paris immediately following the war: her involvement with the great writers of the century, her literary struggles, her political views, and her activity in the feminist movement. I wasn't upset to trade the Chilton for the Somerset; the food there is superior, and they serve the best French wines in Boston.

I didn't offer to meet Eliza at the Chilton because I knew she had a routine when she came to Boston. Almost every morning, she went to the Boston Public Library, and I suspected she would stop at the Boston Athenaeum, where she would use their extensive library before arriving at the Somerset. Eliza Stein had decided to live in New England, as many other American and foreign writers had, not only for the tranquility and the stimulating atmosphere here, but also for its many libraries and their voluminous archives. She used them excessively for her research. Since she gave up writing novels a long time ago, she now devoted herself to producing monumental biographies. During the winter months when the snow forced her to stay inside her house in New Hampshire, her work was very prolific. She spent hours at her two working computers, surrounded by files of information, her warm teakettle, and several opened boxes of chocolate that, for years now, had replaced cigarettes.

Once we had set the date, I requested it as my monthly day off, the one the Bank of Boston grants to its managerial staff. I decided to walk from Commonwealth Avenue. The splendid February morning was cold, but the sky was radiant, so I left early to take advantage of the nice weather. I was also thinking that, before going to the Somerset, I would stop at Wiener's. The antiques dealer was located across from the State House and a few minutes from the Somerset. I had seen a pair of gilded bronze andirons I liked very much, and I felt like finding out how much they cost.

As I left my apartment to go to Commonwealth Avenue toward Arlington Street, I was dazzled by the sparkling brightness emanating from the Public Garden and the Common. They were covered with a beautiful snowy carpet of white and were encircled by a bright red border created by the brick houses on Beacon and Tremont Streets. Teenagers were skating on a frozen pond. Young children were playing around a snowman wearing a straw hat. Others were sliding down Telegraph Hill screaming with laughter. This was not Albert Goodwin's rainy, sooty, gray, and sad Boston

I was looking at. It was more that of the winters painted by Childe Hassam, Edward Simmons, or Edward Boit: a joyful and bright Boston, full of life with people happy to be alive. I considered Goodwin equal to Thomas Sargent: Goodwin as the best artist of the city of Boston, and Sargent as the best artist of Bostonians. I only stayed a few minutes at Wiener's because the andirons were already sold. In spite of my detour through the Common and my stop at the antiques dealer, I arrived at the Somerset just as the clock was striking noon. In Boston, to be on time is to be on time.

Of all the clubs in Boston, the Somerset is the most elegant and the most ceremonious. I was greeted by a tall, haughty maître d', thin and even paler than the club members. He led me to a small living room facing the garden; it was obvious this area was most likely designated for guests who were not members. The larger parlor on the ground floor was a reading room where club members came daily to quietly peruse their newspapers without being disturbed. The parlors, as well as the dining room that opened to the garden, were furnished and decorated as a private dwelling. Unlike the other clubs in Boston, the Somerset has maintained the appearance of a fine residence. The Saint-Botolph Club with its art exhibits, the Harvard Club equipped with a gym, and the Tavern resembling a café do not have the dignity and relative intimacy of a family home, or of an opulent Bostonian domicile that the Somerset has.

I sat in an easy chair next to the window and ordered a sherry from the waiter who, after a long wait, had come to ask me if I wanted something to drink.

At the end of twenty minutes I was surprised that Eliza had not arrived. Like me, she was never late. The waiter who had brought me the drink was standing behind the door. I beckoned him and told him I was waiting for Mrs. Stein with whom I was having lunch. He replied that he had not seen anyone.

The wait seemed long, and I started wondering if I had the wrong day. I checked my calendar. It was definitely Tuesday, and I had noted "Lunch at the Somerset with E.S." I decided to go look in the dining room to see if Eliza had gone there directly upon arriving, although she didn't usually do that. When she was at the Chilton, she always waited for her guests in the parlor as she would have done at her home in New Hampshire. The old Bostonians, with a subtle smirk on their European faces, were in the main dining room at noon, savoring their exclusive membership privileges; they didn't even look up as I penetrated their spacious inner sanctum. I returned to the small parlor telling myself that I had waited long enough and it was better to leave a note for Eliza and go home. I had already composed it in my mind: "I am sure that nothing has happened to you, but I think that the Somerset has made an arrangement with the devil to prevent you from seeing me."

I had just returned to the place in the small parlor assigned to me, ready to write my message, when I saw the waiter who had served me the sherry approaching. He whispered in my ear that there was a lady who was waiting for me.

"But where is she?" I asked him a bit abruptly. "I just came from the dining room and did not see anyone."

"If you would kindly follow me, I will show you, sir," he replied curtly.

After walking quite some distance on the first floor, we arrived at a small plain door that opened to a narrow wooden staircase leading directly to the basement. I now realized that you had to be familiar with this building in order to find access to the lower level, where there was another dining room. In Boston the basements, or lower levels as they are known, are sensibly elevated and have windows so that you can still see people passing by on the sidewalk, albeit only their lower bodies.

In spite of a low ceiling and average dimensions, the dining room seemed large and welcoming. A dozen tables were covered with white table-cloths, and the several crystal sconces attached to the walls mirrored and diffused a gentle light that softened the telltale marks of time. Seated at the tables were women, only women, who seemed to be engrossed in conversation. At first glance, the room appeared to be animated, noisy, and gay. At the back of the room I recognized Eliza, wearing an imposing black hat.

She was sitting next to a fireplace with burning logs, but when I got closer, I realized they were electric logs. She had been waving vigorously ever since she had seen me come in.

"But I have been waiting for you for almost an hour," she said, pretending to be scolding me and exaggerating somewhat. "I was beginning to get worried. I was wondering if I had the wrong day."

As I was trying to explain the saga of my long wait in the small parlor, my concerns that something had happened to her, the haughtiness of the maître d', the deliberately slow pace of the waiter bringing the sherry, and the indifference of the Brahmin gentlemen in their spacious dining room, Eliza started telling me in an enthusiastic and victorious tone: "The Supreme Court has just decreed that discrimination against women is forbidden, and that applies to clubs such as this one. So, from now on we shall be admitted to the Somerset. We are given this dining room for lunch today, but now women will be allowed into the main dining room for dinner, if they are accompanied."

The idea of a separate dining room for women seemed quite subtle. The thought that this practice is what made the Somerset especially charming was entertaining to me, and I expressed that sentiment to Eliza. It requires audacity and finesse to obey the law and submit to the injunctions of the Supreme Court, while preserving the old customs and pretending to adapt them to the demands of the times. In Boston the old traditions, which are nothing but outdated habits, have an almost indestructible force. They are the powerful and gentle brakes that can thwart equality. Furthermore, we can count on the reinforcement of Boston elitism to curb the advancement of equality, a boring subject indeed.

These gentlemen from the Somerset knew very well how to get around social equality, and I asked myself if they were looking instead, through subtle means, to skirt another issue unique to the United States: the powerful influence of women. Hermann von Keyserling, in his book *Psychanalyse de l'Amérique* (originally published in English as *America Set Free*), makes a pertinent point on this subject that is still valid today. He says that because the American woman is fundamentally materialistic by nature, she pushes man to concentrate on the acquisition of material goods and to work hard, thereby leaving him with only a minimum amount of freedom.

At the Somerset, in this protected and exclusive enclave of the familiar past, men had found a possible escape from the domination of women. For a brief time they could feel emancipated and laugh about it. They were at ease when they were with each other. Furthermore, during this solitude that had been conceded to them so grudgingly, they could share heaps of little secrets, dreams, and expectations.

As we left the premises, the strength of old habits humbled Eliza, and instead of going through the waiting room and entrance on the main floor, I was surprised to see her proceed toward the small basement door that also led directly to the sidewalk on Beacon Street, as though she thought things could never be otherwise.

9

A BOSTON LADY

Because my bed was placed right up against the window and the shades could only be lowered halfway, all I could see upon awakening was a small edge of the snow-covered Public Garden, a patch of winter sky, and beneath the slanted roofs of Commonwealth Avenue, a peek at the first few floors of the Ritz-Carlton Hotel.

Since arriving in Boston I hadn't had the time to rearrange my bedroom. Cold air streamed in through the window next to my bed and froze my feet, and the city lights forced me to wear the eye mask I had taken from the airplane. In spite of these inconveniences, I didn't feel like moving the bed because I liked the view from this location. It reminded me of Peter Vanderwarker's photos that show the old Boston juxtaposed against the Boston of today, the present projected on the past, concrete towers dominating, but without crushing, the brick and sandstone mansions of Back Bay: all had changed, but nothing had changed.

It was a Sunday morning in January. There was no traffic, and it was as if the city were asleep under a blanket of snow that had fallen heavily in recent days.

I didn't feel like getting out from under my blankets and even less like going into the mess I had left in the small cold kitchen to make my usual Nescafe, which I found nauseating by the end of the week.

I had gone to bed late because I had spent a good part of the evening finishing the report for the bank that was due the following day. It was a grueling project. My mediocre knowledge of economic and judicial English made the task even more difficult. When my linguistic problems became truly serious, I could always phone André, a French expatriate like myself, who worked in an attorney's office. André had access to and could research the best translations, and he was always happy to help me.

The Ritz-Carlton was just a few blocks away from where I lived; I only had to cross Commonwealth Avenue to reach Arlington Street. I had gone there several times for a drink at the bar or a quick lunch, but never for the brunch that my Boston guidebook described as one of the best in the city. In fact, I had never tried brunch anywhere. The American habit of dealing with a boring Sunday by eating twice as much had never enticed me before. But today, after several days of solitude and work, I needed to see people. I also felt like eating and drinking copiously. The idea of going to the Ritz gave me the incentive to get out of bed. I suddenly realized I was starting to think like Bostonians, by dropping "Carlton" after the word "Ritz."

I took a shower, shampooed, and dressed quickly. However, knowing that the Ritz maintained all the old traditions, I carefully chose a necktie. In a very short time, I was on Commonwealth Avenue, reinvigorated by the electrifying brisk, dry, slightly exciting air of winter in Boston.

When I arrived at the Ritz, I immediately went to the small shop where they sell newspapers. I thought I would find a French newspaper I could read, or pretend to read, during my brunch, even if it were a week old. But on the shelf reserved for the foreign presses were German, Italian, and Spanish newspapers; I even saw some in Greek and Arabic, but I couldn't find a single French title. So I had to be content with buying a pack of cigarettes—Marlboro Lights. Then I checked my overcoat at the cloakroom before going to the dining room on the second floor.

The dining room was very brightly lit—all the crystal chandeliers shone as if it were dinner time. Enormous buffet tables were set up in front of the high windows facing the Public Garden. They were covered with silver serving pieces and elaborate food platters, and decorated with gigantic swan ice sculptures. Most of the dining tables were already occupied, many taken up by entire families and people from Beacon Hill. I recognized several I had met since my arrival: the Kanes and the Colliers, who were part of the same family; the Gregorys and the Wicks, whom I had met at the *Alliance Française*, and who were sharing a table; and Eleanor Bleakie, surrounded by her three sons, who were as elegant as their mother. The maître d'hôtel found a place for me in the recess of a window where there were two small tables. One was already occupied by an older woman and a younger man. When I sat down at my table, they were talking very loudly and laughing, looking at me as though they knew me. The woman smiled at me, and her companion gave me a stiff and formal nod. I nodded in return thinking that I must have met them at one of the many Christmas receptions I had attended, but at that moment I couldn't identify them. However, the woman's dark, brilliant glance and the insistent, amused manner she had of looking at me wasn't completely unfamiliar.

I took the menu that had been placed in front of me, and retrieved the sad pack of Marlboro Lights and my old lighter from my pocket. I did this slowly in order to gain some time, hoping that I would remember the names of my neighbors in the interim.

But she was the one who turned toward me and said in impeccable French: "A few years ago I would have asked you for a light to start a conversation. These days, people are less romantic, but I must tell you that, although I dislike rules, it is absolutely forbidden to smoke here."

Then in a burst of laughter, she added, "I must also tell you that we know each other. Oliver (I understood that was the first name of her young companion) and I met you at the Christmas reception given by Mrs. de La Fage. It was barely a few days ago! It's true that there were a lot of people, but have you forgotten me so quickly?"

Listening to her deep, distinct, well-modulated—although a bit affected—voice and scrutinizing her face, I recalled immediately the image of this couple that had struck me when I first saw them. Her appearance was changed today by the black felt hat that encircled her forehead like a tiara. This woman, who was definitely over sixty, and this young man accompanying her, who could have been her son, were a handsome and strange couple, mingling easily and glibly greeting other guests. I visualized them instantly, both of them, at Mrs. de La Fage's Christmas reception that had preceded the one at the *Alliance Française*. It had been an evening attended by all of Boston's Francophiles, chicly dressed, smiling, and bowing somewhat pretentiously. I heard the hostess making the introductions in a very precise and emphatic manner: "This is Dora Reed, director of public relations for Cabot Corporation, the well-known publicity firm in Boston. Dora is also a diligent member of our *Salon Français*. She volunteers to read theatrical selections from our French repertoire." I now remembered very well that upon seeing the young man, Mrs. de La Fage hesitated; her mind went blank trying to remember his name, which she had forgotten or simply didn't know. Stammering she added: "And Mr. ...... who......who is a friend of Dora's," then adding in English, "Her escort tonight."

After the usual greetings, as we were going toward the immense parlor where the large group of invitees had already gathered, Dora Reed had asked me the first and only question of the evening: "Do you like to dance?"

I also remembered that, while taking the young man's arm to join the group of friends who were beckoning to them by raising their champagne glasses, she added, "You know, you need to know how to dance in Boston. That is how we spend our time and keep warm because the winter here is so long and cold."

Now that the memories flooded my mind, I was able to regroup and say sincerely, "I have not forgotten you, Mrs. Reed." I pronounced her name with emphasis to show that I remembered her. "As a matter of fact, I was thinking of coming to listen to you at the next *Salon Français*."

To show that she too was not fooled by anything, Dora Reed replied briskly, "Well, start by joining our table. It will be more pleasant!"

I accepted her invitation and had no sooner sat down than a waiter, dressed in a white jacket decorated with big gold epaulettes, brought me a flute of champagne. It surprised me a little that they would serve champagne for breakfast, even if it was closer to noon. Dora Reed noticed my reaction, and bringing another glass of champagne to her lips, she said, apparently amused, "In Boston, we submit to this ritual that comes from New York. You must find it rather unrefined, but because I adore champagne, I adopted it immediately."

Dora Reed's companion stared at me. At that moment his eyes appeared harsh, almost mean. Then he fixed his gaze on my tired face, as if he wanted to emphasize its paleness and the dark shadows under my eyes, drawing attention to his own superior physique and at the same time showing annoyance toward his friend who had invited this Frenchman they hardly knew to their table. After a moment, he said in French, with that strong Boston nasal accent, "Foreigners always have trouble adjusting to our climate. Why don't you have a glass of bourbon? There's nothing like it to put you back on your feet."

Mrs. Reed dryly interrupted, "Oliver, it's time to go get dessert and let Monsieur begin his brunch."

As Oliver got up, I noticed his tall stature, his well-cut blazer slightly tailored at the waist, which accentuated a well-developed torso and big shoulders. He carried himself in a nonchalant manner as he respectfully went to pull out Mrs. Reed's chair. When she stood up, she appeared to be shorter than the first time I had seen her, but she was still as elegant. I thought that, as a true Bostonian, it must only be on weekends that she wore flat shoes. Under her black velvet jacket she wore a white blouse buttoned at the neck and a long gray and black checkered skirt that reminded me of a Burmese longyi. When she laughed again, saying, "In winter I have an appetite like an ogre, but at night, no matter what the season, I eat like a poor man,"

I noticed that her fresh laughter, unaffected compared to her voice, helped to make her appear much younger.

The three of us headed toward the buffet. Dora Reed and Oliver exchanged a few words with the people I had greeted when I arrived. Our plates laden with food, we returned to the table. The guilty conscience I would have had on any other occasion by carrying a plate overflowing with cold cuts and delicacies seemed to disappear at the sight of my companions, who had not hesitated to combine large portions of pudding with a variety of French pastries on their plates.

"You know," said Dora Reed, taking her place at the table, "I invited Oliver to this brunch at the Ritz to celebrate a lawsuit that I just won! My lawyer phoned me last night to give me the good news."

I thought she was talking about a lawsuit against her landlord or some tenants, unless it was against an ex-husband for failure to pay alimony, which seemed more plausible.

I saw Oliver turn red, which surprised me somewhat, as if his companion's confessions about her legal problems and their financial implications were inappropriate and embarrassed him.

"So, my dear Monsieur," continued Dora Reed, "I have won my suit against my employer! He wanted to let me go; he had decided to replace me with someone younger."

I understood immediately why her remarks, expressed so candidly, made Oliver feel uncomfortable: they only served to point out their age difference and perhaps, his dependence on Dora. Were we to understand it was a material dependence? Had she drunk a bit too much champagne? Did she want to let Oliver know that she accepted their situation without the least bit of shame? Had she perhaps initiated this lawsuit for him? To show him that she was still young and wanted to enjoy life? Through this lawsuit, he too would be a winner.

Dora Reed continued to laugh, and between gulps of champagne she added, "Three months ago I received a letter from the president of my company letting me know that the administrative board had eliminated my position because they wanted to institute a new policy. For that they needed someone recently graduated from college, closer to the needs of the personnel. I must admit that they offered me a very generous exit package."

Oliver interrupted her by slamming the table with his fist and whispering exasperatedly, "Dora, everything is settled now, so let's stop talking about it."

She pretended not to hear and continued. "I believe that my president, who is an extremely miserly man, could not accept that I took Thursday afternoons off. I had told him about it because I don't like to lie. I made up for this absence by going to the office every Saturday morning, but that wasn't acceptable because he didn't actually see me there. For him, Saturdays are sacred; he goes skiing in Vermont. For me, it's Thursday afternoons that are sacred. I love to dance. I come to the tea dance at the Ritz every Thursday afternoon, and nothing will make me change my routine."

I ventured to add, "I see that there's a true incompatibility between the two of you."

"Well, my dear Monsieur," continued Dora Reed, her face flushed from drinking champagne and the anger she felt toward her former boss, "He has paid dearly for his letter. As you know, in the United States, the law forbids the use of a person's age to fire someone, and this legislation is strictly enforced in Massachusetts. I filed a suit against him. I won it, and my exit compensation has actually been doubled."

Drawing confidence from Dora Reed's report of the lawsuit's happy conclusion, her victorious tone of voice, and the relieved expression I could now read in Oliver's face (who must have been wondering if his friend had not gone too far with her revelations), I ventured to affirm in a judgmental manner, "Boston women are always the first to fight against discrimination. They have always contributed to the advancement of women's rights. With the free time you now have, you will be able to pursue other interests."

"I am counting on it, and I plan on seeking a new position. I have already sent my resume to several companies," she explained. "While waiting I'm going to dance a lot. You must come with us. You will see there are many balls in Boston all winter long. Personally, the one I support is the Silver Ball. I also help my old friends, Suki de Brangaça and Elaine Uzan-Leary, to organize the *Alliance Française* Ball that will take place in April. They have christened it *le bal du printemps* in contrast to our winter balls and snow balls. It's one of the most successful dances in Boston and is held at Faneuil Hall. Many Harvard students attend, and it's very festive."

"I don't know how to dance very well," I responded. "I took a few lessons when I was a student but had to give them up to prepare for my exams. I learned a little bit of the waltz, polka, and also the paso doblé. I believe they would come back to me easily enough."

"But that is very good," said Dora Reed. "I adore the waltz, and I also love the paso doblé—nobody in Boston knows how to dance the paso doblé."

"Is the Boston still danced here in Boston?" I asked, pronouncing "Boston" with a French accent.

"Hardly ever because we still remain somewhat puritanical. It was a marvelous dance and so elegant, less intoxicating than the Viennese waltz. I am delighted that you know how to dance the real dances. I am always the first one on the dance floor. Ah! The lambada—what audacity! But to waltz is something else. We have the opportunity to waltz all winter in Boston, thanks to Miss Libby and Mrs. Whitelaw, who organize a cotillion at the Copley Plaza Hotel. I will introduce you to them. I'm sure they will like you, but they are very particular when it comes to attire. Miss Libby and Mrs. Whitelaw require men to wear a white tie and the young ladies, a white dress with long white gloves. They do not waver on this point. They can give you the name of a dance instructor who will come to your home to help you brush up on your waltz."

"Why don't we invite Monsieur to help us prepare for the Silver Ball next week?" added Oliver, who seemed to be more at ease when the conversation changed from the realm of litigation to the dance floor, making him more pleasant toward me all of a sudden. His eyes, harsh and almost mean a little while ago, had become soft and slightly childlike now that the talk was more peaceful. When he smiled, the dimples in his cheeks accentuated traces of his boyhood that had been preserved in his facial expression. He had a charming way of smiling; it was a winning smile.

"I don't know if I would be very useful to you, except maybe to stuff a few envelopes, send faxes, and make a few phone calls," I responded.

"Dora would never forgive you if you didn't come to give us a hand," said Oliver. "As for me, I'm in charge of seeing that the dance floor at the Copley Plaza Hotel, where the Silver Ball will be held, is perfect, without the slightest roughness, smooth and slick like a mirror. Dora wants it to look like the ice skating rink at the Public Garden."

"Yes, that's true," said Dora. "When I was a child there was a small orchestra playing next to the ice pond, and that's where I learned to waltz. We lived in Back Bay, and my father took me there every Sunday. My father was a true Bostonian. He wasn't afraid of anything, and he loved the winters. There were some winters when I saw him skating on the frozen Charles River! The dance floors are paramount for our balls, and every year I must fight against the invasion of carpeting: the American hotels love to put it everywhere."

Then suddenly becoming more serious, Dora Reed added, "If the waltz evenings are boring for you and if the afternoon dances at the Ritz are not your cup of tea, at least come to a ball where you will be contributing to a good cause: the Silver Ball is given for the benefit of the Children's Hospital."

I saw Dora pick up her napkin, hardly unfolded, put it on the table, and take her handbag. Curiously, it was a tapestry evening bag that she had placed under her chair. She adjusted her beret in a manner that displayed small wisps of hair on her forehead and temples and proceeded to get up slowly, very slowly, as if she were being filmed. "Oliver and I finished our brunch and have prevented you from having yours. We're going to go now and leave you alone. Oliver must get to his sports club to work out as he does every Sunday, and since he's abandoning me, I'll go to the two o'clock movie at the Nickelodeon by myself. They're showing *A Room with a View*. I liked the book very much, and they say that James Ivory's film is excellent."

When I saw them going toward the grand staircase, crossing the now almost empty dining room, Dora was clutching Oliver's arm very tightly and she seemed frail, small, and somewhat stooped next to his tall, sporty frame. She made me think of a seagull. She had that piercing look, like a seagull a little weary of swooping and guiding his companions down to earth. But toward what port was she leading Oliver?

I didn't go to either the tea dances at the Ritz or the Viennese waltzes, but I did go to the Silver Ball. I said I didn't have the time for the other two. I was pleased to meet my new friends there. I felt that a friendship was developing between us. Basically, I admired them. I was attracted by their beauty, their slightly eccentric elegance, their extravagant manners, the disparity between them, their nonconformity, and the compulsion they had to be different. That said, they also scared me a little.

In the immense Hall of Mirrors at the Copley Plaza where the Silver Ball was gearing up, Dora and Oliver were busy greeting everyone, going from one group to another. From their table, right next to the dance floor and to which I had been assigned, I could confirm that Dora's wishes had been granted: the dance floor appeared to be even smoother than the skating rink at the Public Garden. Oliver, in his white tie and tails, was superb. He wore them with natural ease, like a prince accustomed to wearing official regalia since childhood. Dora was stunning in an airy black tulle dress, her waist cinched with a large maroon taffeta belt and an immense white ostrich feather in her hair, which was coiffed in a chignon. Dora granted me the first dance. She waltzed marvelously.

Then several weeks passed, and I didn't see them. I thought of phoning but I hesitated, not wanting to bother them. One day in February—it must have been the end of February because the days were longer—I met Mrs. de La Fage on my way to the Ritz to buy a pack of cigarettes and asked for news about Mrs. Reed.

"But it's awful," she said. "Didn't you hear? Dora had a terrible automobile accident. The pavement was covered with black ice, and the car skidded out of control. Miraculously, Dora was unharmed, but the young man, you

94

know, the tall young man that always accompanied her and whose name I don't recall, was killed instantly."

"Are you talking about Oliver?" I asked.

"Yes, that's it. Dora had just bought him a car—one of those sports coupes hardly made for this area—with the money from her lawsuit."

10

THE BLUE DINER

Almost every week Mike, Dick, and I had gotten into the habit of going to the Regatta Bar, the jazz club at the Charles Hotel in Cambridge. We would go to the first show at eight o'clock so that we could finish the evening someplace else.

The show at the Regatta was mediocre that night. None of us liked the tenor, who was rather phlegmatic. As for myself, I had difficulty understanding him because of his New York accent.

Mike suggested we go to the Willow in Somerville instead. Perhaps it was because he wanted to enliven the atmosphere that was becoming dull. It was his favorite club, a venue for true jazz fans. Frankly, neither Mike, Dick, nor I felt like taking the detour to get there.

Dick was quiet; he appeared sullen, which seemed to happen often. Mike didn't say anything, brooding because we hadn't wanted to take his suggestion.

I suggested we stay in Cambridge and go to Night Stage, another jazz club not very far away. According to the calendar section of the *Boston Globe* that morning, Stan Getz was performing his first concert there after a long hiatus. Dick and Mike agreed. We also agreed that the saxophonist ranked among the greatest jazzmen, but I sensed the Brazilian rhythms of Stan Getz wouldn't be enough to cheer up Dick.

The Charles Hotel valet arrived with Dick's black Buick. The body and fenders were shining brightly, and only the tires had some mud on them. Dick wanted his car to be impeccable. Even in winter he waxed it more than necessary to obtain a perfectly smooth and mirror-like glossy black finish. It was icy cold outside, so, as we rushed to the car, I glanced at the winter night sky—transparent, bright, and overloaded with stars. It reminded me of the movie theaters of my childhood whose dark navy blue ceilings were studded with tiny lights.

Mike insisted on taking the back seat. I sat next to Dick, who headed in the direction of Night Stage, but by way of Harvard Square, because plans can always change. From the Charles Hotel we quickly came onto Boylston Street by going behind the new buildings of the Kennedy School. Dick turned left toward the Harvard Square newspaper kiosk, which was teeming with people in spite of the late hour. Then, after following Harvard's brick wall, he turned right onto a wide and deserted Massachusetts Avenue. He was still quiet. He turned on the radio and inserted a cassette into the tape deck.

I immediately recognized Saint-Saëns' organ symphony. That was easy for me because Dick played it often. Of all of Saint-Saëns' music, I only knew *The Carnival of Animals* that was often played at the Sunday Concerts Colonne. When I was a child, my father would make my sister and me stay in the house and listen to it while it was broadcast on the radio. Dick seemed to like this symphony very much, and I was beginning to get interested in the competing sounds between the organ and the piano.

For Dick, it was another way of making Mike, and especially me, understand that there was a kind of music other than jazz. Dick said there was too much freedom in jazz, and that from time to time, you had to return to things that were less abstract, which for him signified things that were more orderly.

Without saying anything I silently approved of his choice. Saint-Saëns' symphony went well with the burst of winter that night, a high wind coming from the ocean, impetuous and vehement, sweeping Massachusetts Avenue of all its human lava. Dick was right. The Saint-Saëns symphony, strong and clear, perfectly composed and conducted, brought your mind back to where it should be. Dick often said that getting your head straight was the only thing that mattered. The scheme of the symphony spoke to me; it re-established its almost violent equilibrium and vigor and made me think of some *Preludes* by Liszt.

Talking to Dick, who pretended not to hear me, I said that when we listen to this symphony, we feel like getting up, going further, going faster, and accelerating the passage of time and events.

Dick stepped on the gas. The dreary facades of Massachusetts Avenue unwound before us at top speed, and in the blink of an eye we were at Cambridge City Hall. All of a sudden, with a sharp turn of the steering wheel, we saw empty taxis hurtling down Mass Ave eager to go home. Then he took a small street on the right that led to Memorial Drive. We had passed the street for Night Stage a while back. It was obvious that we wouldn't be there to welcome the return of Stan Getz.

Dick knew Cambridge like the back of his hand. He had lived there for ten years. He liked Cambridge a lot; he said that one was freer and more peaceful there than in Boston. After finishing at Harvard, he had settled there as a lawyer. It was at the end of his studies for his law degree that he met Jackie, who was finishing her music program to become a teacher. After their marriage (I believe that Jackie was Dick's one and only love), they lived on Arrow Street for a couple of years, next to Saint Paul's Church. Dick was even a Cambridge selectman for a while.

When Jackie left after their breakup to live in California permanently, Dick moved to the South End in Boston. He justified the change by saying that he had been too happy in Cambridge to stay where he had lived with Jackie.

I recall one evening, after just the two of us were at the Regatta Bar, Dick took me on the itinerary he would take when he was married to Jackie. We went from Mount Auburn Street, where his former offices were located, to their old apartment on Arrow Street. He showed me all this without bitterness, almost with joy, as if the fond memories were enough to make him happy.

It was then I had guessed why Dick was so attached to Saint-Saëns' symphony. One night while he was retracing the route of his life in Cambridge, I took the cassette box to see who was directing the orchestra. It was Enrique Bátiz, the head of the London Philharmonic. Dick said to me, "Jackie adored music. That's why she decided to become a music teacher. In spite of the cold and snow that she hardly liked, she came from California to study here in New England. I think she would have stayed in Boston, not because of me, but because of the concerts! And because of Tanglewood! We would go there every summer. We had a marvelous time there last year. It was the first time I listened to the Saint-Saëns symphony with organs. It was directed by a young French adjunct of Seiji Ozawa and had a sort of contained anger. I found it very structured, very strong, as if it clearly announced the stages of destiny. On the way home Jackie explained the scheme to me. She loved French music very much: Saint-Saëns, Fauré, Ravel, and especially Debussy."

Since we were driving along Memorial Drive and had tacitly rejected Night Stage, everyone was silent. The express lane merged onto the route along the Charles and made several loops following the course of the river. At a certain point, the express lane abandoned the river to climb a small hill and arrive at a sort of promontory that overlooked the entire city.

Dick braked briskly and stopped the car but kept the motor running. "We have to listen to the end of the tape," he said dryly while raising the volume as high as possible. He got out of the car, left the door open, and went toward the guardrail. He leaned against it as if he wanted to contemplate the city, shining with a million lights, while listening to the end of the symphony. The wind was brisk. It blew his jacket and his hair and, even without an overcoat, Dick didn't seem cold. His jacket collar was turned up against his neck, and his hands were deep in his trouser pockets.

Leaving the doors wide open so we could hear the music, Mike and I got out of the Buick to join him.

The rhythm of the symphony increased. Suddenly the organ exploded with furor, with a majestic allegro as it pushed back the piano's brief lull to reassure a victorious finale.

Boston's beauty sparkled on the other side of the Charles. The Old Hancock Tower barometer—like a sapphire, yet more brilliant than those found in Mogok, Myanmar—forecast that the evening would be beautiful and clear. And next to Boston University, the gigantic bright red Citgo billboard was blinking like a lighthouse at the entrance of a port. While gazing at the city I thought of the words of Simone de Beauvoir, who wrote in *L'Amérique au jour le jour* that when she flew over Boston in a plane at night, Boston burst before her eyes like fireworks in a bed of golden and multicolored glitter.

Mike and I went to each side of Dick to get closer to him, shelter him, and gather strength from the cold. When I put my arm over Dick's back, I felt Mike's who had the same idea I did. Both our arms were intertwined on Dick's wide and tense shoulders. We stayed like that for a moment after the tape finished, without saying anything, each of us interpreting, before we were to be separated, the message of this city that had united us.

Dick loosened himself from us, took a few steps, then turned around and screamed in anger, "You see, tonight I'm forty years old and I haven't done anything. I've wasted my life and have added to the failure of those who loved me."

I knew that Dick hadn't coped well with Jackie's leaving. Even though their marriage had started to disintegrate several years ago, Dick and Jackie continued to live together without seeking to explain why and how they had arrived at this stage. Dick continued to love his wife without realizing, or without wanting to understand, that she was slipping away from him and sliding down a perilous slope. Although he didn't want to see her fall, he did nothing to hold her back.

When Jackie went to a detox center, he pretended she was taking a short trip with her mother. When she began to see a psychiatrist, he gave her money without asking for an explanation. When she stopped working, he encouraged her to stay home, saying he earned enough money for the two of them.

Their life together, just the two of them, only two because they didn't have any children, is perhaps what suffocated Jackie. Dick had few friends and lived only for her. For many happy years, her husband's presence was enough for Jackie. Then Dick began to work more. He thrived in his work; many clients wanted him to represent their case. His serious approach and success were well known. The more he achieved, the further away he drifted from Jackie.

Dick didn't realize right away that his wife was starting to drink. And when he discovered the truth, he didn't want to face it for fear of reliving, for a second time, the torments that had marked his young life.

He had spoken to me once of his childhood wounds, where the daily conflicts between his father and mother left little room for tenderness. But in the sadness of those days there were some small joys. At night when his father came home, having already consumed a good deal of alcohol, his mother would rise up in anger. Dick told me he would take his father outside and ask him to take a ride in the car together. He would help him to hold the steering wheel straight, he would tell him to slow down at the curves, and he would even slip his leg between his father's to apply the brakes. He liked these escapades because he felt responsible for their safe return; they served to sober up his father and calm his mother who, upon their return, could see from her kitchen window that the car had not been damaged.

Dick had been impacted twice in the same way. For him, life was repeating itself.

The Saint-Saëns symphony had stopped now. There was only the night's silence enveloping the Charles River flowing toward the ocean without remorse, calm and satisfied with the route traveled. Our own quiet thoughts and solitude were all that was left. We sought to conquer them through the connection that life and this city had allowed us, as if giving us a second chance. On the other side of the river the city lights invited us to continue our trip, to cross the bridge and rejoin the community of human beings.

Dick, now calm, got behind the steering wheel once again, while Mike sat in the back seat and I took the one next to the driver.

Dick said that he was only acting as our chauffeur but, to tell the truth, he wouldn't have minded this type of work. He knew how to drive with speed and flexibility. Because the whole area was so familiar to him, he was able to select the quickest routes. His car, always perfectly waxed, was irreproachably clean on the inside; he vacuumed it almost every day. It was forbidden to smoke, eat, or drink while traveling with Dick, which was real torture for Mike, who loved to ride around with a Diet Coke in his hands or licking an ice cream cone. He also said he would have liked this kind of work because you had to be silent: a good chauffeur does not speak, and passengers shouldn't talk to the driver.

Turning toward Dick I said, "What if we went to get something to eat to celebrate the birthday you kept a secret from us? It's too late to go to Night Stage now, and I feel like I have a hole in my stomach."

"At this hour there's only Bertucci's or Café Budapest," responded Mike.

"Don't you have a better idea?" I said. "Pizza is too plain for birthday festivities, and the other is too chic for tonight."

"The Blue Diner!" Mike exclaimed all of a sudden, happy about his idea.

"Yes, the Blue Diner seems perfect. We eat well there, and for someone who has the blues, it's the ideal place."

Dick understood the allusion and, shaking his head, he agreed.

We had just passed the MIT buildings; we were on Commercial Street arriving at the Longfellow Bridge, which would lead us back to Boston.

Dick put another tape in the deck to let us know that he felt better. This time it was jazz, the Four Freshmen; we had both heard them at the Regatta Bar at the beginning of the winter. Dick referred to them as *Les Quatres*

Bizuts. He and Jackie had been students in Paris together for two years. Dick spoke French very well and found it amusing to use a few words of French slang once in a while. I always spoke French with Dick but fell back into English when Mike was with us. Dick had bought two tapes by the Four Freshmen that night when we were leaving the concert, and he had given me one. I found the vocal perfection and sophisticated technique of the quartet as well as the sharp, high-pitched voices of the singers somewhat irritating.

Dick had a different opinion. By playing this jazz piece, he wanted to make sure Mike and I, but especially I, understood that in all the bad moments that come our way, there is some light, some small joy, like discovering jazz clubs in Boston and Cambridge every week.

The Four Freshmen continued their number with more rhythm when they took up the old fifties tunes. We started down the Fitzgerald Expressway and were approaching downtown. The Custom House Tower was already visible, strangely dominating the area, looking like a fake Tower of London. Dick accelerated, stepping on the gas full force, and the Buick quickly and quietly passed the massive brick silhouette of the Rowes Wharf Hotel. We soon reached the completely lit up Federal Reserve Bank, whose architectural design formed a large electric H on the night sky, and then arrived at South Station.

After bypassing the train station's rounded buildings, Dick took a diagonal right to Atlantic Avenue and then turned onto Kneeland Street, which borders Chinatown without actually being a part of it. The Blue Diner, a restaurant in the shape of a train car, is parked on Kneeland Street at an angle where it intersects South Street.

On winter evenings like this, when there's been a downfall of heavy snow, the Blue Diner's lowered metallic shades filtered only a single ray of yellow light coming from under the shades. When we arrived, we had a vision of a train car immobilized by the storm and stuck there for the night. I thought of the Second World War and of the boxcars stopped in the snow fields. I could see a small train station lost in the French countryside. I believe it was Vierzon, on the demarcation line between the occupied zone and the free zone. I thought of the long waits in a freezing coach for an identity check and a pass. I thought of my mother, who had covered my sister and me with her fur coat to protect us from the cold, and I relived the fear I felt as the German soldiers were searching our bags. But these long-ago memories that had flooded my mind all of a sudden went away at the sight of the big coffee cup and the large neon-lettered sign on the restaurant's roof. We came back to reality and to the original idea that we had come all the way here to eat well and not spend too much. The restaurant advertises accurately: the Blue Diner fights relentlessly against hunger.

In spite of his less sociable and quiet side, Dick liked to show off how lucky he was, and he also wanted to avoid having his passengers slip and smash their faces in the packed snow. As usual, he had no trouble finding a parking spot almost directly in front of the restaurant.

Mike knew the Blue Diner well. He went there often and he was well known. The restaurant was filled. It appeared to be much bigger and especially much wider than a train car. All the stools around the bar and the tables lined up along the windows were occupied. But the waitress, whom Mike called by her first name, Paulette, told us to wait a few minutes. She was bringing a check to customers who were about to leave.

Mike and Paulette laughingly engaged in small talk. I understood that she lived in Hull like Mike's parents and that she returned there every night after the restaurant closed. She didn't come back to work until the following afternoon at four o'clock. She said she didn't mind because she could take advantage of the beach and the fresh air all day and could even walk by the ocean.

She was a petite brunette with a sparkling look on her square, clear face. And when Mike asked her if she liked her job, she answered in French with a strong Quebecois accent, which to me is always like a fresh burst of optimism: "There are nice people everywhere!"

I was happy to hear her say that. Certainly, all her ancestors from Quebec wouldn't have survived the harsh American winters if they hadn't had the strength of their language and culture to make them feel good, keep them unified and committed to preserving their heritage.

Because Mike had most likely told her I was French, Paulette turned toward me and said in French, "Did you know there is a small French cemetery in Hull? There are Frenchmen who died there following an epidemic. They had come to fight on the side of the Boston insurgents."

"Yes, I'm familiar with it. I went there with Mike's parents."

Paulette seemed somewhat surprised by my reply. The French are very forgetful. She seemed amazed that a Frenchman of this day and age would know of a small cemetery at the top of a cliff overlooking a rarely used beach south of Boston. At the crux of the dunes among the wild gorse and high grasses lie a handful of Frenchmen who had given their lives to defend America's freedom.

Mike always established a spontaneous and warm relationship with those who worked in the cafes and restaurants he frequented. He had an immediate connection with them; he knew what their work was, that it was better to be in a good mood no matter what kind of problem you had in order to earn the money you needed. Mike had worked in several restaurants in Boston before he could apply to Merrimack College. He had fond memories from that time. He had quickly earned enough money to pay for college; he had made several good friends he had kept up with, while he had lost contact with all his college friends.

Mike began to talk of his memories about that time in his life, which turned into quite a long monologue. "There were some nice chaps at the Meridien Hotel where I worked the longest. We would meet two or three times per week and almost every Saturday. We didn't ask many questions, we accepted each other as we were, we helped each other out. There were Dean and Buddy, who I still see. There was also Roberto Celli, who disappeared. Dean was a little older than the others, and after being just a waiter, he became a professional barman because the maître d'hôtel noticed that he was quick and always smiling. The women found him very appealing with his very dark hair and eyes and his 'black Irish' complexion. Even though we didn't live in the same area, Dean would often drive me home after the restaurant closed. He would say: 'Don't spend half of what you earned tonight by taking a taxi. I'll drop you off.' He would insist: 'It isn't a chore for me, I love to drive at night, and with the bad weather we have now, the cops are not out.' He would leave me at my door on Isabella Street, which created a long detour for him, and then go back to Charlestown, where he lived in a small house all by himself on the docks where the Charles and the Mystic Rivers merge. Sometimes I go to the Copley Plaza bar to have a drink, listen to Dave McKenna on the piano, and see Dean, who has become the head barman there. He hasn't changed."

Mike continued his reverie. "There was also Buddy, Buddy Campbell. With a name like that, you can't forget him; besides, he often left his name on my answering machine. We were both students; he was at the University of Massachusetts studying law. He wanted to become a lawyer, but since his parents didn't give him a single cent, he worked in several restaurants such as the Meridien. That's where I met him. Buddy spent a lot of time juggling his class schedule and his work hours at the restaurant. Frequently, because of a late class or an exam he had to study for, he would call to ask me if I would fill in for him. He didn't want to lose his job. Nevertheless, Buddy was well organized. He had a girlfriend who would come to get him by car every night that he worked. Later, and for a quite a while, Buddy would telephone and ask me how things were going. He would call from his office at Blue Cross Blue Shield, where he had become a director in the large health insurance company."

Mike finished the story of his restaurant friends by talking about Roberto Celli, who had disappeared without giving any sign of life. "Roberto came from an Italian family fresh off the boat. He hadn't gone on to further his education; he worked in a funeral home as a chauffeur. Between the two services at the church and at the cemetery, during those off-peak hours, he spent his free time at the track, where he gambled a lot. He only came to the restaurant at the Meridien intermittently, to recoup. He was generous. He always bought a round before last call. One night, after some champagne, he left, and we never saw him again. Dean told me one day that Roberto had gone to Los Angeles and had been hired by a funeral home there; but he noted that Los Angeles also had one of the most beautiful race tracks in California."

When we sat down at the table Paulette was setting for us, with a little bit more attention than usual, as if she wanted to be more gracious to us than to the other customers, I thought that we all had the same idea. Each of us was saying the same thing to himself: we had to seize the few moments that God had granted us now, to breathe somewhat, to warm ourselves and to stick together because we would not have them for very long.

We had crossed a city that was a vast desert of stone. We had ridden along the void by crossing the suspension bridge (was it the Tobin Bridge?). After crashing into a pylon (was it on the side of the Mystic River, where it joins the Charles?), we had spent some quiet and anxious moments listening to the end of Saint-Saëns' symphony in the harsh wind while looking down on the black foaming water and the city of Boston illuminated by thousands of lights. But, in his mercy, God wanted, and there was no doubt we were in agreement about this, that all three of us would find each other on this winter's night, survivors in the shelter of a train car that was going nowhere.

We had to thank God before taking up the paths that would separate our lives, perhaps forever, as if they didn't belong to us. We were going to leave each other; we were going to go off in different directions. My training at the bank lasted only a few more months; the end had been determined in advance. I felt Mike was ready to imitate Roberto and try the California adventure, and I knew he would do it. And Dick? His roots were in Boston. He was proud of the city, and he also had memories here. Dick would stay; he would continue to work hard to succeed and to forget.

We had to be grateful and thank God.

11

REMEMBERING SARAH VAUGHAN

I heard about Sarah Vaughan's death while I was in a taxi going to the Center for European Studies at Harvard in Cambridge. Raoul Girardet was giving a lecture on *La droite en France*.

The taxi driver seemed to be listening to the daily news on the radio without thinking about what was being said. The volume was so low, as if it were just for him, so I asked him to turn it up a bit. I couldn't hear well in the back seat, and I wanted to make sure I hadn't been mistaken. No, I hadn't.

The announcer was talking about the different stages of Sarah Vaughan's career: her beginnings with Earl Hines, her recordings with Charlie Parker and Dizzy Gillespie, her meeting with Miles Davis, the creation of her own trio, and her appearances with the greatest symphonic orchestras in the United States. He concluded by saying that, along with Billie Holiday and Ella Fitzgerald, her rich contralto voice and the wide diversity of her vocal techniques ranked her among the best jazz singers of our era.

She was nicknamed "The Divine One." Her face was haughty, square, perfectly framed, with large eyes heavily made up with a deep blue eye shadow that was almost green, a boldly outlined mouth with bright red lips, short, glossy black hair, and a smooth and wide forehead. I could envision her as she appeared on the jackets of her records, her compact discs, and her cassette tapes—a face bursting with light.

I never had the opportunity to see her on stage. She no longer performed live after she became ill during the 1980s. It had been a long time since she had appeared in a jazz club or at Symphony Hall in Boston.

I didn't know of any other voice that was equal to or could be compared to hers: serious, high, gruff, well-modulated, covering a wide vocal range, and caressing the lyrics of her songs. I started thinking of my favorites: "While You Are Gone," "My Reverie," "Just Friends." They were fresh in my mind: "Thanks for the Memory." Thank you, Sarah Vaughan, for all the memories, the memory of candlelight and wine ....

I had heard these songs recently at the Willow, a jazz club in Somerville that Mike had introduced me to, where a young black singer, straining a bit on the scats but sounding very much like Sarah Vaughan, was belting out her favorites. She even looked like her. When I mentioned this to Mike, I mispronounced the name of "The Divine One." Mike decided to teach me how to correctly pronounce "Vaughan" that night. He insisted that you had to swallow the "gh," accent the first and last syllables by combining and elongating them into one, and say Sarah "Vawn."

"But it's pronounced like Maugham, as in Somerset 'Mawm,'" I replied in surprise.

Mike didn't know who Somerset Maugham was, so I didn't say anything more about the British writer, or about his short stories (which I considered to be the best in his genre), nor of his marvelous travel descriptions of Asia in his memoirs.

As we approached the Anderson Bridge the traffic became heavier, and we were stuck on the bridge for some time. It was rush hour. Cars were jammed together everywhere. We had hardly gone over the bridge when we had to stop again for a red light next to the Weld Boathouse, the Harvard sculling club whose rooftop looked like a frozen snow-covered bonnet. I thought I would be late and would have difficulty finding a seat in the small hall at the Center for European Studies. Seeing I was going to be late anyway, I asked the driver to drop me off at the Harvard Coop so I could buy some Sarah Vaughan tapes before going to the lecture.

It was the end of April, and Sarah Vaughan's light had just been extinguished in California. According to the calendar, winter was over, but this year that was not the case. And like God, who likes to impose pleasure and surprise, winter, with no thought to giving an advance warning, would hit Boston and New England once more.

A fierce blizzard, perhaps the last of the season, had paralyzed the northeastern United States the night before. I had welcomed the storm with joy because I love the snow that is so much a part of Boston. It seemed to nudge the city to curl up into itself. It also filled me with sadness because it reminded me that Bostonians had to survive a long winter every year, but it had been so new and so short for me; it was soon time for my internship at the Bank of Boston to end and for me to leave the city that I had come to love forever.

At the Coop I bought the two albums where Sarah Vaughan sings Gershwin. The small plastic boxes had marvelous titles listed under the shining face of The Divine One: "Embraceable You," "A Foggy Day," "I'll Build a Staircase to Paradise."

When I'm back in my room, I'll be happy to listen to her voice while, from my window, I can gaze at the Back Bay rooftops laden with snow under an almost violet, deep purple Boston sky—just as I have done so many times before.

12

PORTRAIT OF A CHILD

I would always turn onto Charles Street after walking over the Longfellow Bridge and passing the octagon-shaped county jail on my left. According to the local newspapers, the prison would soon disappear and become part of the Massachusetts General Hospital. Coming from the bridge, I would stay on the sidewalk on the right-hand side of the street because that's where all the stores were located: bookstores, florists, many real estate offices, consignment shops, and some authentic antiques dealers. It was the antiques that interested me most. I was looking for a few pieces of furniture for the apartment I had just rented in the Back Bay on Commonwealth Avenue.

Marika was the first antique shop I would reach. I would stop for quite a while in front of the store window. You could see the entire layout of the store and its contents: some English furniture, many paintings, and a few simple Shaker pieces. On the other hand, the window at Samuel Loew Antiques, located farther down the street, displayed only a few items of questionable value to pedestrians passing by. In order to discover all of its treasures, I knew that you had to force the door open to gain access; the old owner was not very kind. Inside there were rare ship models, and since Boston had been involved in the opium trade, there were paintings of Chinese ports, engravings of whalers and their adventures, silver items from the old Massachusetts Bay Colony, and dinnerware from steamship liners. Closer to my apartment, at the intersection of Charles and Mount Vernon Streets, I always stopped in front of the Eugene Gallery. It only had a very small window above its basement level, and there were piles of old bound books and lovely lithographs of Boston that changed often but always remained affordable.

When I came home at seven o'clock one cold December day, Marika, like most of the other stores, was already closed, but the shop was dimly lit by lamps on small tables. Christmas decorations were displayed all winter. Some chandeliers, some andirons, and some Chinese vases sat on a shelf that was decorated with silver paper garlands intertwined with gold-threaded tissue. If you stuck your nose against the window you could see all the paintings that hung on the wall at an angle to the storefront.

The many canvases were hung one on top of the other in tight rows and in no special order. For several weeks, I had noticed a large picture of a child. It was the only portrait among a variety of different-sized still-life paintings and landscapes.

Because the painting was placed a few feet from the storefront window, you could see well enough to realize that it wasn't only a face but a full-length portrait of a child surrounded by a large, heavy, golden frame. It was apparently a nineteenth-century painting, the type of family portrait that was popular during that era: a small boy wearing a dress seated under a tree. He seemed to be holding something in his hand, but it was difficult to guess what it was from the street. Even from a distance, it didn't look like a toy. Was it a flower? A bird? A shell? I was intrigued by what the young boy held so carefully as well as by the expression on his face; he was dressed as if for a special occasion and seemed well behaved sitting in the shade of a big tree in the countryside. I had trouble identifying the background on the canvas. It seemed to be the sky, or maybe it was the ocean.

Because of my work schedule at the Bank of Boston, I decided to return to Marika on a Saturday morning when the store was open to see the portrait once again up close and from inside the store. Besides, Charles Street is more pleasant on Saturday or Sunday mornings, when Beacon Hill residents do their shopping and people from other neighborhoods come to stroll. The street is very animated, cheerful, and bustling with pedestrians. On other days it is empty and quiet. During the week, when I had a few minutes at lunch time, I was content to buy a sandwich at the small store located in the bank lobby and, rather than going to Charles Street, I preferred walking toward Newbury Street, which was always lively and upbeat.

But it was in the evening when nighttime had already wrapped itself around Beacon Hill that I liked Charles Street best. Walking almost the entire length of the street on my way home to Commonwealth Avenue every night, I noticed its mystery and felt its bewitching power. Just like Commonwealth Avenue, Charles Street reveals its mysterious beauty in the solitude of a winter night: deserted, battered by snow, and streaked with banners of fog where, just like real gas lamps, the street lights are softly reflected in the facades of the brick houses. Charles Street reverts back to its old self, noble and secretive, turned inward, as it must have been in another era when Charles Dickens hurriedly walked along this same stone pavement to Jamie and Annie Fields' house. I also knew that Charles Street could have another side to it. It had been several years ago that Albert DeSalvo, the "Boston strangler," had roamed this same old street during his grotesque murdering streak. He would watch for his prey, nurses from the neighboring Massachusetts General Hospital going home at the end of a day's work. The police had found blood stains on the snow.

One Saturday morning I entered Marika's. Because the two sales clerks were at the counter helping other clients looking through a box of jewelry, I went directly to the portrait hanging on the wall next to the window facing the street.

It was truly a large canvas; it must have measured more than five feet tall and at least three feet wide. The corners of the very ornate gold frame were damaged, but the canvas was intact and the colors, although a little old, remained beautiful. The child's dress, dark blue, cinched by a wide yellow-and-red striped silk belt, had been painted with care. The child's face, above a large white pointed collar, was perfect. It was a picture of a small boy, about six or seven years old, with full cheeks and blond curls cascading onto his shoulders. He had a gentle and dreamy expression. In his left hand, I was surprised to discover, was not a flower, or a bird, or a shell, but a watch, a large pocket watch with a long gold chain that wrapped around his arm and fell onto his knees. It was not a child's watch. It was an adult's watch, maybe one that his father had loaned him to distract him so he would sit still during the many long hours of posing. Perhaps once the artist had finished the painting, his father would let him have it as a reward? Getting closer to the painting, I noticed that you could read the time that was precisely painted on the face of the watch: it was eleven o'clock. The artist's signature, H Falkland, and the date 1848, were written in black at an angle in the right corner of the canvas.

I liked the painting. I thought it would go well in the parlor of my apartment with the maple woodwork and the few Victorian pieces of furniture the landlord had left, most likely because they were too cumbersome to move to another place. He had left nothing on the dark wooden walls except two or three twentieth-century engravings of the port of Boston. The large gold frame, the soft colors on the linen, the discreet but real presence of the child would be enough to revive the living room.

I could envision it above the fireplace in the parlor. It was the perfect place for it in this Back Bay apartment that was built at about the same time the picture was painted. With this portrait, I would accentuate the Boston aspect of the living room, with its bow window defined by drapes, its sculpted woodwork, and its tall white marble fireplace, which I realized would be poorly suited to modern paintings. Anyway, I didn't feel like modernizing it; just the opposite, I took great pleasure in reconstructing the old Boston atmosphere.

Did I have other reasons, other motives besides decoration for wanting this portrait? Actually, and without admitting it to myself too much, I would have liked to know why this child was holding this big watch, which obviously was not his. The child himself must have known. He must have known why he had turned the watch facing outward, as if to let the person who was painting his portrait know what time it was.

I said to myself, "If the painting costs under $1,000, I'm buying it."

I approached one of the two sales clerks who were behind the counter. He was carefully replacing the old jewelry pieces he had just shown to a young couple in their appropriate boxes; they apparently left the store without buying anything. I asked for the price of the portrait that had been displayed for some time and that couldn't seem to find a buyer. The clerk said he didn't know but would ask his boss, who was negotiating the cost of an old mirror with another young couple.

The owner left his clients for a few moments and came to tell me, "It's a nice painting and in good condition. It's signed by Falkland and was exhibited at the Dublin Exposition in 1850. It goes for $2,000, but since we've had it for some time I can give it to you for $1,500."

It was a lot for a painting that would certainly have a beautiful effect but whose value, other than maybe the gold wooden frame, seemed relative to me. Antiques dealers always have an overflow of portraits, and his price far exceeded what I expected to pay.

"It's a bit expensive for me. I'll think about it," I replied.

I tried to persuade myself that I had to give up this purchase. What would I do with this painting once I returned to Paris? It would be disproportionate in my Paris studio, even with the frame removed and the canvas placed directly on the floor against my white book shelves, which were primarily for paperbacks.

For the last time, as I was leaving Marika, I glanced at the wise child seated under a tree holding a pocket watch with a long chain wrapped around his arm and who was watching me leave with that soft and dreamy look that now seemed to be an air of regret.

I continued on my way to Back Bay.

Scenes of my own childhood came to mind. I could see myself in the schoolyard, my checkered apron buttoned down the back, my curly hair falling onto the nape of my neck, standing apart from the games with a pensive expression on my face. Later, I could see myself at bigger school, in another schoolyard, still without trees but much larger. I was wearing a navy blue sweater, short navy blue velvet pants, and long gray woolen stockings. I could see myself on a winter day in a small study hall with three or four classmates who, like me, excused from gymnastics, were grouped around a red-hot coal-burning stove. One of us was responsible for lighting it at regular intervals to keep it going. I could hear myself reading *David Copperfield* in French, my voice loud and clear, separating each syllable as I had been asked. Father Pierre must have liked my voice because he always selected me to read out loud. While I was reading I would quickly glance at the old teacher who, from behind his thick glasses, would give me a small smile expressing his approval, or maybe it was to show his appreciation. Since he had become almost blind, this hour of supervising a few pupils was the only assignment he was given.

My admiration for Dickens, who was also a winter-night child, dates back to this period in my childhood. I took advantage of my stay in Boston to follow the path the writer himself had taken during his visits here. Dickens liked Boston very much; at that time it must have seemed very English to him since it had not yet become the big American metropolitan city it is today. In return, he was very well liked among the Bostonians, who, recognizing him as he passed by, were enraptured by his European yet somewhat gaudy elegance. I passed by the Parker House Hotel where Dickens had stayed. He must have been dazzled by the comfort of hot and cold running water in the bathroom. Then I crossed Beacon Hill up to Pinckney Street to stop on the south hillside in front of the house of the editor Thomas Aldrich, where Dickens had celebrated a memorable Thanksgiving. Continuing to Charles Street, where his old friends the Fields had lived, I was now not far from my apartment in Back Bay.

During the following weeks, while walking down Charles Street on my way home, I couldn't go by Marika Antiques without stopping in front of the window to look at the portrait. The child with the pocket watch was always there, in the same place, in the middle of paintings of floral bouquets and pastoral scenes. He exerted the same power over me, the same force that first attracted me. I kept saying to myself, "It still isn't sold; most likely it won't sell because this type of painting isn't in style anymore, and it's too large for today's homes. Only family would have kept it. In a while I'll go back to the store to negotiate the price."

One night, it must've been the end of March, as the days were starting to get longer, I had trouble crossing the Longfellow Bridge because it was snowing and there were strong gusts of wind. As I approached the Marika window display, I could sense that something had changed, something that concerned me.

I immediately noticed that the display wasn't the same. The Christmas decorations that had been there all winter had been removed. The Chinese fans had been replaced by andirons, and there were old silver frames where the Chinese vases used to be. I hurriedly looked for the portrait of the child.

On the right-hand side of the wall, still crowded one against the other, were the same paintings, but I couldn't see the portrait, that unique painting. It had been replaced by the scene of a somber, almost black stormy seascape. With my face against the window pane, I searched the entire store for the portrait. The inside didn't seem to have changed; everything was intact. On the back wall above the wooden counters, the usual tapestries were hung, and against the left wall where the entrance was located, the same heavy mahogany or walnut wardrobes that were of interest to no one still stood. As usual, a small table and two or three Shaker chairs as well as several odd armchairs were displayed in the middle of the store. As must have happened every year at the end of winter, only the shelf had changed, and the portrait of the child was no longer there.

I was momentarily upset by its disappearance, telling myself that I was wrong not to have taken it, knowing especially that the dealer would certainly have lowered the price and would have accepted monthly payments. I resigned myself to thinking that finally this child could not come home with me. He had probably left Ireland and its tragedy, most likely his native city of Dublin. He had arrived in Boston safe and sound, and now it was better that he remained here. In New England he could find a wealthy Irish family, peace, calm, quiet, and happiness, and he would be less disoriented. Also, as he did in Ireland, he could see the ocean, the countryside, and the fields at the water's edge.

I felt like going back to Marika's to try and find out something about who had bought the painting. They certainly wouldn't give me the name of the purchaser. American merchants are too respectful of their commercial laws. But I was starting to know the antiques dealer and his two sales clerks. Perhaps they would give me some information that would allow me to learn more about the adoptive family, their age and social standing, and, if I was lucky, to know if they lived in Boston or the suburbs.

I returned to Marika the following Saturday morning. As usual the store was filled with people at this hour. Several young couples were at the counter having jewelry boxes opened for them. Adjacent to it, the owner was behind a small table and was sorting some papers. I didn't dare disturb him. I walked around the store and stopped at the large marine-scape that replaced the space left by the portrait. It certainly was dark and sinister, truly representing a shipwreck, drawn and painted with excessive violence. I quickly turned away from it and went toward the two sales clerks who were now free and said to them, "You remember that portrait of the child that I liked so much? It's too late now that I've made up my mind to buy it; it looks like it's been sold."

"It often happens like that. I see it many times with the jewelry. People hesitate and pass up an opportunity and then later regret it."

"I'm curious to know what kind of person could buy such a large painting. You would need to have very large rooms for it to show well."

The clerk replied that he didn't know, and that I could ask the owner about it. He was the one who had made the sale.

The old antiques dealer had been listening to the conversation while sorting his papers. He raised his eyes and said, "It's a young family from Beacon Hill who took it. They're furnishing a weekend house they've just purchased on Cape Ann. They both liked the portrait and are thinking of putting it in a guest room."

I limited my reply to, "It's true, these portraits of children are especially decorative."

After a brief silence and looking at me more cautiously, as if he were going to reveal some precious information he wouldn't have told anyone else, the old shopkeeper said, "Because they inherited a lot of furniture and paintings from their family, they first of all wanted to see if the portrait would go with their new house and the furnishings they were planning to keep. If it doesn't fit, we agreed they could return it."

My heart quivered hearing that the portrait of the child might return to Marika and come back to me. I knew it was a dream, and there was little chance it would come true. Besides, there was every reason the portrait would go perfectly in the summer home by the ocean north of Boston owned by the young Beacon Hill couple. The lovely house, whose walls were covered with ivy, was on the North Shore, as the Brahmins affectionately called it. It would be in the middle of a garden of big oak trees like the one the child was leaning against in the painting. After crossing the ocean and a long wait in the store that had welcomed him, the child had found a definite refuge in a family whose social milieu was similar to his. With the optimistic but unrealistic conviction of someone who throws a bottle into the sea, I said to Marika's owner, who by now had gone back to his writings, "Here is my telephone number. If ever they change their mind, would you let me know?"

I would continue to walk down Charles Street but no longer stopped in front of Marika's display. I would, however, quickly glance toward the window. Nothing of the new decor changed. Nothing had changed on the wall of paintings.

For my parlor, I ended up buying a federal-style convex wizard's mirror topped with an eagle, the symbol of the United States. I had found it in one of the many secondhand dealers along the route to Cape Cod. I hung it above the white marble fireplace. At dusk, the mirror reflected mauve stains, the Back Bay rooftops, and, on certain evenings, a brick-red light of the sunset coming from the west, reminding me of a large forest fire.

BOSTON, MY BLISSFUL WINTER

One evening, coming back to my room after working late, my eyes burning with fatigue and my head feeling heavy, I suddenly became dizzy, so I approached the fireplace to lean against the mantel. I noticed my reflection in the warped mirror, but, in a sort of fog, my own face vanished, and in its place, I seemed to see that of a child with blond curly hair, the face of a young boy with a soft and thoughtful look. It was me when I was a child.

Quite a few weeks later while I was in the middle of packing my suitcases, packing last-minute purchases, gifts, and the last of my souvenirs, I received a telephone call. It must have been the month of May because the magnolias on Commonwealth Avenue had already bloomed, and Boston was alive with the joyful noise of the many college and university commencement celebrations.

It was the owner of Marika. "I am calling you about the portrait. After keeping it for quite a long time, my customers have just returned it to me. They finally decided that the painting didn't go in their new summer house. Are you still interested?"

I didn't have much time to think about my answer. I had to suppress my surprise and contain my joy. But my happiness was not the same because since my last visit to Marika things had changed for me. I answered, "I am just about to move, I will be leaving Boston in a few days. I thought I would stay an extra year, but I received a new assignment and I'm packing my luggage."

"Do I understand that you're no longer looking for the painting for your Boston house?"

"That's right. I don't know how my new home will be."

"Well, all that's left for me to do now is to wish you a good trip."

"No, no," I said in a single breath. "I will take it anyway. It'll keep me company. I'm taking it."

"As I promised, you can have it for $1,500."

"That will be fine. You can have it sent to me at Commonwealth Avenue. I will send you a check today."

After a few minutes of silence, the antiques dealer added, "I think it would be better to make a wooden container so the canvas and the frame won't be damaged during your move and during the trip. I'll have it made and will pay the expenses myself. I can have it delivered directly to your forwarding agent; that way you won't have to worry about it. You must be very busy preparing for your departure."

I hesitated a moment before answering:

"I won't see the child in the portrait before leaving Boston, but I accept your kind gesture. I'll send you my forwarding agent's address. Thank you again for thinking to call me."

Then I went back to organizing my things. The parlor was already emptied of the few pieces of furniture that I had bought during my stay. And I had already rehung all the engravings that belonged to the landlord. But there were still several boxes to fill, of books that I always took with me, of letters kept in their envelopes that, for the most part I didn't reread, of old unsorted files that I left closed. All these things followed me everywhere. From now on, many of the tapes I had bought in Boston or that had been given to me would become part of this ambulatory heritage.

To give myself courage I selected a tape of George Benson, *Weekend in L.A.* I would play it often when I was in a good mood, when I was happy. It stayed on my playlist for a long time. I loved listening to the stimulating rhythms, the marvelous full and punctuated tones of the orchestra, and the warm voice of George Benson.

I felt something pleasant was about to happen, and my heart skipped a beat; all of a sudden I had a vision of the child in the portrait showing me the hour of the large pocket watch he was holding. It was as if he wanted to remind me that it was now time to leave, to go far from Commonwealth Avenue, far from Back Bay, far from Boston. He was also telling me that his destiny, now very clear to me, was that wherever I went, he would be at my side to give me the time and to guide me in the right direction. Whether I found myself in countries with people of other colors, of other knowledge, in the lands of other faiths, in godless parts of the world, in police states or in sectarian cities, he would continue, in his innocence and truth, to give me the time: Boston time, where there is a reasonable and tolerant world.

The splendid and rough Boston winter that seemed so short had hardened me. And the people of Boston had taught me so many things. More than anything else they had taught me that the willpower, the force of the spirit, and the enthusiasm with which we undertake to do what we must do, and to do it as well as we can, are what lead us through the challenges of life and make it more beautiful.

I felt strong enough to leave once again.

Rangoun, August 1994

AFTERWORD

I've just read an interview in the *Boston Globe Magazine* with Alain Briottet, Consul General of France, who was about to leave his post in Boston to become the French Ambassador to Burma. He stated that the one thing he would miss the most about Boston was the snow, everything associated with the snow, and winter …. "Your mind is lucid and more able to deduce what to do. It's a very good season to work," said Briottet ….

I agree, and should I ever leave this place for a warmer climate, I, as well, will miss the winter most of all. Winter forces everything inside. It invigorates. You think twice before you go outside. You cannot move freely from the inside to the outside. You have to stop and put on more clothes, then you have to stop and take them off when you get to where you are going. There's nothing casual about winter in New England ….

Winter does have its setbacks, however. Thoughts driven inside sometimes go round and round, getting nowhere. We can often create problems and questions that aren't even there if we stay too long inside. I'm sure this is why God gave us seasons: winter to be inside, summer to be out, that we might understand the patterns and processes of life ….

John Fisher
Making Real What I Already Believe
Bethany House Publishers
Minneapolis, Minnesota, USA

ABOUT THE AUTHOR

Alain Briottet devoted his life to a career in French diplomacy. He served in Europe, America, and Asia, and held several positions in collaboration with the French Ministers of Foreign Affairs in Paris and throughout the world. *Boston, un hiver si court* (published in English as *Boston, My Blissful Winter*), a series of 12 short stories, is a reflection of his appointment in Boston during the 1980s as Consul General of France. He later served as French ambassador to Rangoun, Helsinki, and Dacca, the Organization of the Caribbean States, and the Antilles-Guyana Zone. In 2001, he oversaw the coordination between the Ministry of Foreign Affairs and the parliamentary mission investigating the events of Srebrenica. In 2016, he published a novel devoted to his father, a French officer and prisoner of war in Germany: *Sine Die, Gross-Born in Pomerania*. Among his many awards, Alain Briottet was honored as a Commander in the French Legion of Honor, an Officer in the Ordre National du Mérite, Chevalier des Arts et des Lettres, and received an Honorary Doctorate from Assumption College in Worcester, Massachusetts. He currently lives in Paris.

ABOUT THE TRANSLATOR

Paulette Boudrot (Letendre, Johnson) was raised in Fall River, Massachusetts. She earned a BS in Education from Bridgewater State University, an MA in French Language and Literature from Middlebury College in Vermont, and a diploma in Twentieth-Century French Literature from the Sorbonne, University of Paris. Paulette taught French and ESL in elementary schools, colleges, and universities throughout Massachusetts and Rhode Island. During the 1980s, she transitioned from education to administration of French Cultural Services at the French Consulate in Boston. In 1995, she founded PLJ Administrative & Business Solutions, a company outsourcing administration and project management for small to medium-sized companies. An active member of Rotary International, Paulette resides on Cape Cod in Massachusetts. *Boston, My Blissful Winter* is her debut novel translation.

ACKNOWLEDGMENTS
BY THE TRANSLATOR

There are so many who have supported me along this journey of my first literary translation. My appreciation goes to the author, Alain Briottet, for reading the first chapter, and then directing me to "Continuez!"; my daughter and author, Alison McLennan, who is an inspiration by example; the workshop participants at the first Middlebury Bread Loaf Translators Conference and our workshop leader and translator, Maureen Freeley, whose invaluable advice to join the American Literary Translators Association led me to several conferences where I learned from many like-minded members, especially Joyce Zonana and Ellen Elias-Bursac.

I would be remiss if I didn't mention Melissa DeMarsh, Margaret Collins Weitz, Mary Louise Burke, Lia Poorvu, Patricia Sullivan, the late Maureen Yazbak, Brian Michaud, Ann Menashi, the late Pauline Nelson, Emily Balistrieri, and Elizabeth Buddy for their input, edits, and enthusiasm for my project.

This publication would not be possible without Lucinda Clark, founder and owner of P.R.A. Publishing and fellow Rotarian, whose belief in this story and whose persistence encouraged me to move forward. Thank you to P.R.A. Publishing Assistant Laura MacDonald, for working with me on details, and especially to Christie Lowrance for her last-minute rescue.

My editor, Ellen Albanese, deserves the highest kudos for her skill, expertise, and professionalism in putting the finishing touches on this book, and especially for her friendship.

Finally, I am most grateful to my late husband, Richard, for his patience, understanding, support, and encouragement.

CPSIA information can be obtained
at www.ICGtesting.com
Printed in the USA
LVHW011535130920
665854LV00011B/13

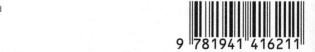